REAL DIRTY

Book One of the
REAL DIRTY DUET

MEGHAN MARCH

ISBN: 978-1-943796-69-4

Editor: Pam Berehulke, Bulletproof Editing
www.bulletproofediting.com

Cover design: @ Hang Le
www.byhangle.com

Cover photo: @ Sara Eirew, Sara Eirew Photography
www.saraeirew.com

Interior Design: Stacey Blake, Champagne Formats
www.champagneformats.com

Visit my website at www.meghanmarch.com.

ABOUT THIS BOOK

I have everything a guy could want—a new single burning up the charts, more money than a simple country boy could spend, and a woman I'm planning to marry.

Until she doesn't show up for my proposal.

The life I thought was so perfect, isn't.

The guy who thought he had everything, doesn't.

I've got my heart on lockdown, but life sends me straight into the path of a mouthy bartender who puts me in my place.

Now the only place I want to put her is under me.

I thought I was done with love, but maybe I'm just getting started.

ONE

Boone

AS SOON AS THE LAST CHORD OF MY BRAND-NEW single dies away, I jam the microphone back into its holder and stalk off the stage, leaving the lights and the roar of the crowd behind me.

Where the hell is she?

"Boone—"

"Great show!"

"Nice job!"

Over the noise of screaming fans, people yell to me, but I ignore it all and head for my dressing room. I don't have shit to say right now.

Only a few people knew about my proposal plans, and I can't stand to see the sympathetic expressions on their faces. I don't need anyone's fucking pity. It's not like I was stood up at the altar. My girlfriend's flight was canceled or delayed . . . and she's not answering her phone. I'll just have to come up with a way to top this one. Somehow.

Amber better have a damn good explanation for where

she is. I know she's independent and just as busy as I am, but that doesn't mean I don't frigging worry when she goes MIA like this.

After shoving open the door with my nameplate on it so hard it smacks into the wall and bounces shut, I flip the lock and lean back against the wood panel.

At least my parents aren't here. Jesus. That would have been more than I'd want to deal with.

They're my parents and I love them to death, but my mom would have alluded to this being the universe's way of telling me I need to think about what I'm doing.

"Marriage is sacred, Boone. Are you one hundred percent sure that she's the one?"

You would think Ma would be thrilled at the thought of adding another daughter-in-law to the family, but it's safe to say she was more excited about me turning down my community-college baseball scholarship to try to make it in Nashville.

When I packed my rusted-out truck with my guitar and clothes, she hugged me hard and dished out her special brand of wisdom. "You do what you need to do, Boone. We'll always be here to support you, and you better believe I'll be first in line to buy your record as soon as it releases."

Ma didn't have to wait in line for shit. I hand delivered the first copy the label gave me to her house before release day, but that didn't stop her from going down to Walmart and buying every one they had on the shelf. All sixteen of them. Because that's my mom, supportive to a fault . . . on everything but this.

Tilting my head back, I focus on the white drop ceiling above me. Normally after a concert, I'm riding high, but tonight I'm off my game because of Amber. It's not every day you have an epic proposal planned and the person you're going to propose to doesn't show.

Someone pounds on the door behind me, and I shove off the wood as it vibrates.

"Hey, man! I got the keys to your ride! Wanna get outta here?"

The voice belongs to Zane Frisco, one of the openers. The crooner with shaggy blond hair picks up plenty of the women I pass on because I'm not looking to cheat. This tour has been a pussy parade that launched his career to the next level.

When I don't answer, he drops his voice. "Vultures are circling. Press must've found out about your plans. Time to roll."

There's no way I'll make it out of this venue without being spotted, especially if the press is foaming at the mouth to get a story. It takes everything I have not to turn around and punch through the door. I flex my hand into a fist. It's been a long time since my tattooed knuckles pounded into anything.

Putting my hand through the panel isn't going to change a damn thing, though. Uncurling my fingers, I turn around and yank it open instead.

Frisco leans with his shoulder against the door and nearly falls inside when it swings wide.

"Thought you were tunneling out under the wall." He straightens and holds up my keys and the pair of brass knuckles that serves as the keychain. "Your security detail is clearing out the press. Thought now would be a perfect time to get the hell out of here."

After a couple of months of touring together, Frisco gets it. Sometimes you just need to walk away from all the shit that goes along with being able to draw a crowd big enough to fill a stadium.

I grab the keys from his hand and we stride back toward the stage where my new obsession waits. The completely restored Olds 442 is as sweet as fuck and was delivered only yesterday. Other than backing her off the trailer and driving into a room for the press to drool over her and then up onto the stage, I haven't taken her anywhere.

I was going to drop to one knee beside her and ask Amber to spend the rest of her life rolling through the back roads with me, but we all know how that turned out.

My fingers tense, wanting to try to get her on the phone, but what would be the point? She's got to be on a plane; otherwise, she would have called me back already. She'll text me from her condo asking me to come over when she gets in.

She didn't know what you were planning, so cut her some slack, I tell myself. I'm trying to give her some grace, but my patience is wearing thin.

Sometimes you just have to roll with the punches, so why not get out of here and put the 442 through her paces?

As soon as I lay eyes on the slick black-and-red paint job, I feel lighter. I jerk my chin at Frisco in the direction of the muscle car.

"Let's go."

The engine growls like the bad bitch she is as I roast the tires in the parking lot of the venue. In my rearview, two men in black suits stand with their arms crossed over their chests, watching me disapprovingly as a cloud of smoke fills the air.

Tough shit. My security. My payroll.

Which means I can do stupid crap like this and they can't say a damn thing.

"You gonna let Tweedledee and Tweedledumb follow us tonight? Or are we gonna act like we got some goddamned balls and go have some fun?" Frisco asks, the taunt clear in his tone as a roadie waves me toward the open gate that leads out of the parking lot.

He's still new enough in the industry that he can go places without being recognized, but I don't have that luxury anymore.

"You know anywhere we can go without being mobbed by people? I'm not in the mood for that tonight, man."

Frisco lays his arm along the open window frame. "I got the perfect place in mind. But first, let's see what this beauty can do."

TWO

Boone

A HALF HOUR LATER, THE SMILE ON MY FACE IS IN danger of becoming a perma-grin.

Damn, it feels good to tear around town in the sweetest piece of American muscle I've ever owned. We only had to duck into one alley to lose a cop, which shows you just how much I've held back. Last thing I need is a reckless-driving charge for the press to chew on and blow out of proportion.

Frisco laughs his ass off as we head back toward downtown Nashville and his apartment. He's got one of those lofts in a rehabbed warehouse somewhere around here.

"Where am I going? Am I dropping you off?"

His laughter cuts off. "Fuck no. That was just the warm-up, right? We need some booze."

I slow as traffic gets heavier near Broadway. All the people crowding the streets reminds me of playing for tips in some hole-in-the-wall on Sixteenth Avenue before

I finally landed a record deal. Everything happened fast after that.

One day I was sleeping in my car, and the next they were putting me up at a hotel I couldn't afford on my own, all because some record exec saw dollar signs when I played.

Worked for me.

"Where we headed?"

"Take a left up here." He points toward a dark side street.

Even though I'm questioning whether he's got his directions backward, I turn.

"Two blocks down."

A few minutes later, the glow of blue-and-green neon lights appears up ahead.

The Fishbowl.

The logo looks exactly like you'd think. A blue bubble of a fishbowl with green writing in the middle and a matching green fish inside.

I slow, intending to pull up to the curb, but he points toward the next side street. "Take a right and park in the back. Might help keep someone from spotting the car and trying to track you down."

"Good looking out."

I guide the 442 around the back of the crumbling three-story brick building and park next to a rusty Javelin. Frisco is already climbing out of the car and shutting the door when I stop and look at it.

"I wonder whose ride this is."

Frisco shoots me a grin. "Only the hottest woman I've met in this town who keeps turnin' me down."

"You fucking serious? We're here so you can try to get laid by some chick who shot you down?"

He pauses, his fingers wrapped around the crooked handle of the back door of the building. "Guess we'll find out."

Frisco yanks it open, and for a second, I consider leaving his ass here and going home. It would serve him right.

The light from inside streams through the closing door, and Johnny Cash's gravelly voice slips out.

What the hell? It ain't like I've got anything better to do tonight anyway.

The inside of the bar is like plenty of others I've been in. Stale aroma from years of smoke hangs in the air of the high-ceilinged space, longer than it is wide. A scarred wooden bar stretches down the middle section of the left wall, probably about thirty feet in length.

The walls are plastered with photos of country legends from a bygone era, and the one nearest to me has an illegible message written to Rhonda above the scrawled signature of Merle Haggard.

Frisco makes a beeline toward the bar where a woman with an incredible rack and a wild mane of dark hair works the taps for two people seated on stools.

She's gotta be the one Frisco's after. I can't argue. The man has impeccable taste.

I tear my eyes off her and survey the only other patrons in the bar. The couple looks like they've been taking up space since Merle signed the picture on the wall.

Frisco may be right. No worries about a security problem here tonight. I doubt Fred and Ethel have ever heard of TMZ or would know who to contact to report a celebrity sighting.

But just to be on the safe side, I tug the bill of my worn baseball cap lower before crossing the scraped concrete floor.

THREE

Ripley

WITH A PRACTICED SNAP OF MY WRIST, I FLIP the tap and drop a hand to my hip as Zane Frisco approaches the bar with his trademark cocky grin. If he asks me out this time, what will that make? Five times? Obviously, it's flattering, but that doesn't mean my answer is going to be any different than it was the last four. I have to give the guy props for being persistent, I suppose.

"Shouldn't you be fighting off groupies backstage right about now?" With a raised eyebrow, I set a pint glass of Miller Lite on the bar napkin in front of Earl before grabbing a second one for his wife, Pearl.

The older couple has been coming to the Fishbowl for as long as I can remember, even back before everything changed. They've seen the good, the bad, and the ugly in this bar, and if I were ever to take Miller Lite off tap, I'm pretty sure one or both of them would die of a heart attack and haunt this bar for the rest of its days. *However few days that may be.*

Snatching up the towel in front of me, I wipe away any stray drops of beer and attempt to shove down the negative thought. The Fishbowl may be a dying tradition, but that doesn't mean it shouldn't be spotless.

Frisco leans forward, his elbows on the bar, and his grin shifts into what I'm sure would count as a panty-dropping smile—if I were the kind of girl to wear panties, that is.

"What would I want with a groupie when I can come here and see your beautiful face?"

He's not short on the charm, but I'm immune.

I drop the rag in front of me and cross my arms under my breasts, not worrying about whether it pushes them up higher under my George Jones *Rockin' with the Possum* V-neck. "Put it in a song, Frisco. It'll get you a lot more play than you're gonna get in this bar tonight."

He shakes his head, keeping that smile intact. "Someday you're gonna say yes to going out with me, and I'll let you apologize for all those times you shot me down."

I don't hold back, dropping my arms and letting my laughter go free. "Points for eternal optimism, but it ain't happenin'. You know my rule. Better men than you have tried and failed to get me to break it."

His cocky grin tilts. "Such bullshit, Rip. You and your rule are about the only things that make me wish I was still playing in bars and crashing on couches, broke as hell. If I'd only known . . ."

Frisco winks at me, and I know he's not taking my rejection any harder than normal. He's not stupid and he doesn't lack for options. He'll probably leave here, stop at a bar with customers who are under the age of seventy-five, and pick up a girl to take home.

And I'll be going upstairs alone again *to take care of business myself*. That's if I don't fall asleep as soon as I climb into bed because I'm running on five hours of sleep total in the past two days. I shut down the momentary flash of fatigue and pin my smile into place.

"What are you drinking tonight, Frisco?"

"The usual. Plus, whatever he wants." Frisco jerks his chin toward the direction of a man stepping out of the shadows near the back entrance.

Crap, I need to change that light bulb. When did it go out? As soon as the thought enters my head, it's replaced by a flash of female appreciation.

Dayum.

Frisco is no slouch in the build department, but the way this guy's broad shoulders, muscled chest, and thick biceps stretch out his faded black T-shirt has all the spit drying up in my mouth as he strides closer.

Wow. That *is a man.*

His battered baseball cap is pulled low, hiding his face, but I can make out the dark scruff of a beard on his chin. My gaze slides down to the ink on his arms, and the parts of me that haven't seen any action in longer than I want to admit roar to life.

My survey drops lower to take in his worn jeans and black shit-kickers before dragging back up to his face just as he lifts his head to meet my eyes.

No way.

Zane Frisco did not bring Boone Thrasher, country music's reigning bad-boy superstar, to my bar.

I've gone too many days without sleep. I'm seeing things.

But when those black motorcycle boots step closer, I know it's not the lack of REM cycles screwing with me.

Boone Thrasher is in the Fishbowl.

"Jack and Coke. Heavy on the Jack."

His deep voice is just as raspy as it sounds on the radio, and my nipples peak.

Nope. Not happening. Danger. Abort mission.

Frozen like a deer in the headlights under his intense blue gaze, I force myself to spin around and face the mirrored wall with glass shelves holding bottles of liquor.

Squeezing my eyes shut, I take a deep breath. *Celebrities are only good for one thing, and that's trouble.* Except . . . with one phone call, I could fill this place with enough women to put the Fishbowl back in the black for the month.

I let the vision play out in my brain.

Instead of gawkers coming to see the bathroom where former country legend Gil Green was murdered, people would be packing the bar, buying drinks, and trying to get close to the country music entertainer of the year.

The skin on the back of my neck prickles and my lids flutter open.

In the reflection, Boone Thrasher's gaze slams into mine. My hand freezes in midair as I reach for the half-full bottle of Jack.

"You trust her?" His words come out as gruff as when he growls into the microphone at his concerts. Not that I've ever had extra cash to splurge on a ticket to one of the big stadium shows.

To the right in the mirror, my peripheral vision catches the blur of Frisco nodding his shaggy blond head, but my attention stays focused on the face beneath the shredded brim of the black hat.

"Ripley's good people. She ain't gonna say shit to anyone about us being here. Ain't that right, darlin'?"

Those blue eyes bore holes in me as my tongue darts out to swipe over my lips while I gather my wits to respond.

I start to speak, but no sound comes out. Clearing my throat, I shake my head first instead. "No one is gonna find out you're here from me."

Thrasher nods at Earl and Pearl. "Can I buy that round for you, folks?"

Earl and Pearl aren't slow, especially when someone is offering to make their Social Security fixed-income budget stretch a little further.

Earl's reflection turns to the certified-platinum recording artist. "You buy 'em all night, and we got a deal. I can play deaf, blind, and dumb. Just ask the wife."

Pearl twirls around on her stool, surprisingly nimble for her age, but what's even more impressive is that her peach-tinted curls don't move at all.

One night after several Miller Lites, she finally let me in on her secret. "Aquanet. Hold down the sprayer until your finger can't take it anymore, and then go for another couple seconds. Your hair won't move for days."

I cringe inside, wondering what in the world she's going to say to Boone Thrasher.

"Handsome boy like you should have a sweetheart keeping you home at night instead of out at the bars. Maybe if you didn't have all those tattoos, you'd find a nice girl. Ripley here could use a date, but she won't take up with no celebrity types. Never ever, not after Rhonda done—"

And . . . that's enough.

I spin around, bottle of Jack in hand, and *accidentally* use it to knock Pearl's Miller Lite over, splashing it across the bar and onto her powder-blue polyester pants.

"Oh my word! Watch what you're doin', girl."

"So sorry, Miss Pearl. All my fault."

Her faded green eyes study my face, not missing my pointed scowl. "Well, I never. What's wrong with you, child? Now I gotta go dab myself off so this doesn't set. They don't make polyester like this anymore." With a huff, she slides off the stool and toddles toward the restroom.

Earl doesn't seem fazed a bit. He holds out his hand to Boone, not even watching his wife.

"Earl Simpkins. That's my wife, Pearl. We're what ya call regulars 'round here."

Boone Thrasher shakes Earl's hand. "Nice to meet you, sir." When he releases it, he chooses the stool two over and Frisco sits down next to him.

No one says a word about the fact that I doused Pearl with beer to shut her up.

Boone Thrasher leans both forearms on the bar and studies me from beneath the low bill of his hat. "How about that Jack and Coke?"

FOUR

Boone

WHERE THE HELL DID FRISCO BRING ME? That's the question on my mind as I watch the dark-haired bartender pour a long stream of Jack over ice before topping it off with a shot of Coke from the soda gun.

Ripley? Is that what the old lady said the bartender's name was? Frisco's attention hasn't left her since we walked into this place, and I can see why.

Her curves are poured into her jeans, and she's all tits, ass, and thick, shiny hair. Basically, the opposite of Amber. My girl is rail thin, like so many women in the industry who feel the pressure to keep any extra pounds off because the cameras will just add them back on. No matter what I say, I can't get her to eat a burger to save her life.

I can't picture this bartender picking at a salad with no dressing or cutting a piece of ahi tuna into tiny bites. No, she looks like she'd just as soon dive into a steak and stab someone with a fork if they tried to take it from her.

The mystery isn't why Frisco wanted to come here, but why she keeps turning him down.

When Ripley slides my drink in front of me wordlessly, she reaches for a pint glass and aims her gray eyes at Frisco. "You sure you want your regular? Last chance to try something different." She holds the glass under the tap and waits.

"Who do you think I am? Give me that Bud, baby girl."

Her fingers curl around the handle and squeeze tight. "How many times have I told you not to call me that?"

In the bar mirror, I catch Frisco's wink at her. "And yet I keep calling you that . . . so who do you think is more stubborn?"

She drops a hand to her curvy hip and stares at him. "When I say no, I mean no, Frisco. I'm not playing hard to get. I'm just not interested."

He slaps his hand against his chest. "Wounded. Nearly mortal. You're lucky I got such a healthy ego or you'd give me a complex."

Ripley rolls her eyes and pulls down the handle to start the glass filling with beer.

The stereo system kicks over to Willie Nelson and I take a drink, appreciating her heavy hand with the Jack as it slides down my throat. I soak up the music and old-school atmosphere as Frisco and Ripley talk. Pearl returns from the restroom and starts up a conversation with her husband about something that happened in 1967.

I let it all wash over me, and the bullshit weighing me down slips away.

So I may not have gotten engaged tonight, but there's no time limit on that. I did, however, debut a kick-ass new single and got to put my sweet new ride through her paces.

The only worry I've got left is what happened to Amber. My phone stays silent in my pocket, and worst-case scenarios play through my head until I push them away.

Two hours later, my question is answered in a way I never could have guessed.

FIVE

Ripley

THE BACK DOOR FLIES OPEN, SLAMMING AGAINST THE brick wall. Unfortunately, it's not a new customer to bring the nightly total of patrons up to five and the current count up to three now that Earl and Pearl have gone home.

No, it's my least reliable waitress.

Brandy Lear has never been accused of being dependable or intelligent, and if she weren't my only cousin, I would have fired her dozens of times over.

It's almost two hours after midnight, so I have no freaking clue why she would even bother showing up for work so late.

"Rip, I need some money." Brandy holds out her hand as she picks her way across the worn concrete floor of the bar on icepick heels.

"*Dirty whore*," a squawking voice croaks out.

"Dammit," I whisper under my breath. Esteban has been asleep long enough in his cage that I'd half wondered if the ancient African Gray parrot had finally kicked the bucket. But no, all it took was Brandy's voice to wake him up.

"The fuck was that?" Boone Thrasher whips around, looking toward the corner of the bar where the voice came from. A huge purple cloth covers Esteban's cage, so he's not readily apparent.

"Shut up, you dumbass bird," Brandy hollers at the corner. With her slurred words and smudged heavy eyeliner, it's clear my cousin decided to go out tonight rather than come to work and earn a paycheck. And yet she's still here looking for money. I wish I could say this is the first time that happened. Cue eye roll.

"*Dirty whore*," Esteban says again.

The parrot has about eighty-two phrases in his vocabulary, and none of them are fit for polite company. For some reason, when a particularly flamboyant celebrity came to the Fishbowl one night about fifteen years ago, he brought Esteban with his entourage. Instead of taking the bird when he left, he gifted him to my mama as a present because she was so amazed by him. Pop was pissed, but Mama convinced him that Esteban would be a great addition to the place.

He's been here ever since.

Despite his shocking vocabulary, I can't help but love him. I mean . . . how could you not love a parrot that drops the F-bomb at least a dozen times a day?

For the sake of business, I do try to keep him quiet at night so he doesn't freak out customers. Once I tried to move him up to my apartment, but he screeched for two days straight until I brought him back down to the bar.

He considers himself some kind of watchdog and actually knows how to bark, which I think is impressive as hell.

I have no clue how old he is, but at this rate, I'm pretty sure he's going to outlive me and the bar.

"Is that a parrot?" Boone Thrasher is off his stool and crossing the room before I can stop him.

Frisco isn't the least bit of help. He's sputtering into his beer, laughing his ass off. He tried rapping with Esteban the first night he came into the bar, but gave up when Esteban squawked, "*You sound like shit.*"

I glare at Frisco, but he just laughs harder.

"Please just—" I start to tell him to leave Esteban alone, but Brandy wobbles on her heels.

"Oh my *God*, am I just shitfaced or is that Boone Thrasher?"

Thrasher stops five feet from Esteban's cage and cranes his head toward Brandy, who already has her phone on and the camera flashing.

I think it's safe to assume he's never coming back here now. Not that I wanted him to. No matter how well he fills out that T-shirt.

For the last two hours, I've been making the least intrusive study possible of the man, and while his face has been lined with tension and frustration, he didn't look downright unfriendly until just this moment.

He closes the distance between him and Brandy in less than a second and rips the phone out of her hand. His fingers fly across the screen, and I assume he's deleting the pictures.

"Can't I have one night of goddamned privacy?" He bites the words out with a glance at me that carries an accusation of betrayal.

Brandy raises both hands in the air before adopting a breathy tone. "Baby, I'm so sorry. I didn't mean nothin' by it. Why don't you just come on home with me and I'll make it all better? You don't ever need to think about that cheating slut again."

The atmosphere in the bar crackles with fury as Boone's gaze shifts to Brandy.

"The fuck did you say?" The question comes out like a growl from between gritted teeth as his chest rises and falls.

Boone Thrasher is not a small man. My best guess, he's six feet tall, two hundred twenty pounds, and when he straightens his shoulders, he looks like he's about to rain the wrath of God down on my cousin for running her mouth.

What is she talking about? I dig through my brain for the celebrity gossip that I try to avoid but seem to absorb through osmosis anyway.

Thrasher has a girlfriend . . . a skinny blonde whose sound is more pop than country. *What is her name?*

Ruby? Jade? Some kind of gemstone, I think.

When Brandy stands there stunned and mute, Thrasher repeats his question with menace. "The fuck did you say?"

Brandy's mouth drops open as she slaps her hand against her push-up padded chest. "No. Way. You haven't even heard, have you?"

Frisco pops off his stool, probably because he's seeing what I'm seeing, which is Boone Thrasher two seconds away from losing his shit.

"Whoa there, Brandy. You might want to watch your mouth when you're talking about Boone's girl."

Brandy, never one to be accused of having excessive IQ points, half laughs, half coughs. "Well, she sure as shit ain't Boone's girl anymore. Amber Fleet married some bajillionaire Hollywood producer tonight in Vegas and told TMZ, aka the whole world, she's gonna be the biggest star on the planet."

"*Dirty whore*," Esteban crows right before the room goes silent.

SIX

Boone

I've never hit a woman in my life, but it takes everything I have to keep myself from slapping the words back between this bitch's tobacco-stained teeth.

"What the hell are you talking about?" Rage vibrates through my every syllable. If she were smart, she'd back away.

The bartender must realize I'm a grenade with no pin, because she comes out from behind her station and grabs the skinny bitch's arm to drag her two steps away from me.

The bitch cackles. "This is priceless. Oh my God, I wish I'd gotten it on camera. I could've made millions."

"Brandy, shut your mouth. Go upstairs and sleep it off in the spare room."

"*Dirty whore.*"

"Shut up, you stupid bird!" The bitch yanks her arm out of Ripley's grip. "Don't tell me what to do. I just came here for money 'cause I'm not done partying tonight. But if he'd just give me back my phone, I'll have every paparazzi in this town here and get my payday that way."

Desperate, money-hungry women are all the same in my book—parasites. I open my hand and her phone drops to the concrete floor.

"The hell is your problem!" she yells.

When I lift one boot and bring the heel down hard on it, her screech morphs into a banshee wail.

"You asshole!" She raises an arm to take a swing at me, but I catch her wrist in midair.

"How much?" I bark the words at her, my jaw clenched.

"What?"

"How much to keep your fucking mouth shut about seeing me here? Otherwise, I'll call my security team, and they'll make sure you don't say a damn word."

The color drains from beneath her overly-bronzed skin before her eyes narrow and turn calculating.

"A thousand."

I release her hand like she's covered in open sores and reach around to pull my wallet from my pocket. Her outstretched hand is already waiting before I've got it open.

Counting off the bills, I drop them into her palm and give her a hard look. "You renege on this deal, I promise I will find you and you'll regret it."

Her bony fingers crumple the bills into her fist. "Nice doing business with you, *Boone*."

"Get the hell out of my sight."

Without a look or a word to Ripley, Brandy stomps out of the bar, slamming the door behind her.

"*Dirty whore*," the bird calls after her, but even that can't pierce through the fury and disbelief gripping me.

I stalk back to the bar and pull my own phone from my pocket.

The screen of my phone is packed with notifications. Texts. Missed calls. Messages. I bypass them for the gossip site. One search is all it takes to see that Brandy was telling the truth.

AMBER FLEET MARRIES HOLLYWOOD PRODUCER IN SURPRISE VEGAS CEREMONY

I hurl my phone at the wall with the strength I used to reserve for pitching a strike, and it shatters against Hank Williams's face with a roar that drowns out Kenny Chesney's lies about no shirt, no shoes, and no problems.

For fuck's sake, why would you do this, Amber?

SEVEN

Ripley

THE BOTTLE OF JACK IS EMPTY, AND FRISCO PUSHES himself to a standing position. He spent an hour on the phone talking to people about the situation while Boone Thrasher sat at the bar in silence, pouring liquor down his throat.

The man is going to be hurting tomorrow, and not just his pride. I've spent enough years behind the bar to recognize a wicked hangover in the making.

"You done, man?"

It's my job to assess how hammered someone is before they leave my bar, and Frisco's slurred words and sloppy movements tell me that he's blasted too.

"You want me to call you both a cab?"

Boone finally speaks. "I got a car." He wrenches the keys from his pocket, and something goes flying before pinging against the concrete floor when it lands.

My eyesight is far from perfect, but the meteorite-sized stone on that silver circle means it's obviously a ring.

Oh my God, was he going to propose to his girlfriend?

The question slams into me harder than Boone hit the whiskey.

That would make sense why he got so pissed and then went quiet. I let the possibility turn over in my head a few times.

Wow. Wouldn't that be a kick in the balls? You're planning to propose, carrying around a rock big enough to anchor a boat, and your girlfriend gets *married* to someone else.

And this, my friends, is why I avoid celebrities at all cost. Their lives aren't normal, and I want nothing to do with the craziness that clings to them like ticks on a hound.

Boone stumbles across the floor to retrieve the ring, but instead of shoving it back in his pocket, he crosses back to the bar and slams it down on the wood.

I wince, hoping it didn't scratch. Then again, what does it matter to me?

"Here. I think this'll more than cover the tab for tonight." He waves toward the stools where Earl and Pearl sat earlier. "And theirs."

Jingling the keys in his hand, he says to Frisco, "Let's get out of here before the circus shows up."

While his attention is momentarily distracted, I snatch the keys from between his fingers, and he whips his head around to look at me.

"What the hell? Give 'em back."

I shake my head. "No can do. Dram shop law. If you drive away from here and kill someone, I'm gonna get sued because I overserved you. So you're just gonna have to take a cab or call for a ride."

Boone lunges across the bar toward me, but I'm sober, which means I'm faster and in better control of my body.

"I'll lock them up and make sure you can get them tomorrow if you're sober."

"Come on, Rip. We'll be fine."

I shoot Frisco a dirty look. "No way. Call a cab or get a ride. There's no way I'm letting either of you act like a dumbass when it's gonna blow back on me. Should've picked a different bar, boys."

Boone whispers something under his breath, but I don't catch it.

"*Crackerhead*," is Esteban's less-than-helpful contribution to the conversation.

Frisco laughs at the bird's outburst, and Boone aims a killing glare in his direction. Frisco tries to shut down the laughter but barely contains it.

The country superstar finally looks at me, really looks at me. His blue eyes blaze with rage and pain, cutting into me. I hold my breath, waiting for him to speak.

The question he asks takes me by surprise.

"Would you ever marry a guy while you were dating another? Because she ain't the first one I've known to do it."

My answer, as stupid as it may sound, is honest. "I'd have to date one first."

Boone huffs out a sound that's supposed to be a laugh, but comes out more like a grunt.

"Too smart for all of us." He turns to Frisco. "Get us a damned ride. I'm done. Fucking done with all of it."

"On it, man," Frisco says, finally containing his mirth and lifting his phone.

Boone meets my gaze for another beat. "Anything

happens to my car overnight, I'll own this bar. Get me?"

I slide my fingers into the brass knuckles on the key-chain and make a fist before reaching under the bar and pulling out a baseball bat. "Threaten me again and I'll break your face."

"Told you she was a feisty one," Frisco says to Boone, and I roll my eyes.

Ten minutes later, the back door of the bar closes behind Zane Frisco and Boone Thrasher as they go outside to meet their ride, leaving the ring on the bar.

Just one more reminder why avoiding celebrities is the smartest thing I've ever done. Now, where do I put this freaking ring so Brandy doesn't find it and sell it?

EIGHT

Boone

I ROLL OVER WITH A SLEDGEHAMMER CRASHING INTO MY skull, my stomach rolling, and my mouth drier than the Afghani desert we landed in for my last USO tour.

What the fuck happened last night?

Last time I woke up in a bed I didn't recognize, I swore it would be the last time. I jerk my head from side to side, hoping I'm not going to find a head of hair on the pillow next to me that doesn't belong to Amber.

I did my manwhore stint just like every guy does when he hits it big and all the women come crawling out of the woodwork, wanting to jump on your dick just because you stand onstage and sing. But no more. I've got a woman, and I'm faithful. No loopholes, no *if she doesn't know, it didn't happen*. I don't cheat because I'm a better man than that.

Bits and pieces of last night filter into my brain, and I work on fitting them together.

A parrot.

A gorgeous brunette.

Amber getting married in Vegas.

I bolt up to a sitting position, my head throbbing like it's being crushed in a vise and my stomach liable to revolt at any moment.

Amber got married in Vegas.

No. That didn't really happen. I drank too much and my mind is screwing with me.

I search the nightstand, but my phone is MIA. I shove my hands into the pockets of the jeans I'm still wearing and come up empty.

Hank Williams's face flashes through my mind, and the vision of my phone shattering against it.

Fuck, that means it really happened.

Amber Fleet, my girlfriend, is now another man's wife.

It's not a bad dream or some kind of sick joke. It's my screwed-up reality.

I roll to the side, my feet finding the floor, and steady myself before standing. Doesn't matter how many hangovers you've had, they all suck.

From outside the door, which I now remember is in Zane Frisco's loft, I hear a low, angry voice. I push it open and glance out into a large brick-walled room. Frisco is on his phone arguing with someone.

"No way. No one knows he's here. You send them, the press will be on their ass and he'll be hounded."

When I step out, the hinges creak behind me and Frisco looks up.

"Who is it?" I ask.

"He's up, Nick, you want to talk to him? Because I'm not playing telephone with you two."

Nick Gaines, my agent. Someone must have told him

that I left the venue with Frisco last night.

I hold out my hand for the phone, and Frisco tosses it to me with an apologetic look.

"Sorry, man. Press is having a field day with this shit."

"About what I expected. Not your fault."

It's Amber's. Even though neither of us voice the words, I'm pretty damn sure we're both thinking them.

I lift the phone to my ear. "You got Thrasher."

"Couldn't you have picked a starlet with bigger tits than ambition?"

"Watch your mouth, Nick. I don't care what she did, but you don't get to talk about Amber like that."

He sounds shocked when he speaks again. "You're defending what that bitch did?"

"No. But I'm still not letting you talk shit about her. You wanna be pissed about it? Get in line. I'm the one whose girlfriend didn't bother to tell him that she was gonna elope on the night he planned to propose."

Nick releases a long sigh. "The press is losing their shit with this. They're making it sound like you're the jilted groom and she's the skank-ass ho who couldn't keep her legs closed—their words, not mine. At least you've got sympathy on your side. She just kissed her career in country music good-bye. No one will touch her after this. Word is that her label is already looking at the contract to decide if they can drop her today."

Sympathy? I don't want anyone's fucking sympathy. All I wanted was a damned woman of my own who could hack living this life with me, and the hope of having a family. Just a fragment of something *normal.* Like my folks have. Like my brother has.

Instead, I get this.

If I had taken that community-college scholarship to play baseball, I bet I'd already have a wife and three kids by now. Instead, I chased my dream, and now I'm the dumbass Amber Fleet jilted.

Who uses the word jilted *anyway?*

"What's the plan, Nick? I know you've already got one."

My agent huffs out a laugh. "That's what you pay me for. You're gonna ride this wave for all it's worth."

I open my mouth to object with a *no way in hell*, but he keeps going.

"I know you don't want anyone feeling sorry for you, and you'd rather crack some skulls, but here's the thing—you're going to make one statement. A classy, sincere statement wishing Amber well in her new relationship, and then you're going to step away and go back to doing what you do—pour it all into the music. The press will keep going with the story, and I'm sure Amber won't be smart enough to shut her mouth, but by the time you finish this next album, people are going to eat it up. They'll want to see this side of your music, and you'll have another platinum on your hands."

I let his words and predictions wash over me and say nothing.

Of course, for Nick, this is all about the money. The fact that my pride is taking a beating doesn't compute.

Wait, why didn't I say my heart *is taking a beating?* That's a hell of a good question, and one I don't have the time to answer right this moment.

"What do you say, Boone? We got a plan? I put together a statement, we release it to the press, and then you can stay out of sight behind the gates of your house, shoot some shit, race some dirt bikes, and write the album that's going to have you set for the rest of your life."

I turn his suggestion over in my head. Release a statement to the press. That's not me.

"I want a press conference. I'm gonna have my say."

"Boone, that's a bad idea. If you let your temper—"

"Set it up, Nick. You work for me. So set the fucking press conference up."

With a long sigh, he goes silent for a few moments. "This could backfire and screw up all the plans I worked out."

"And if you think I'm the kind of guy who's going to go hide behind a gate and just *release a goddamned statement*, you still don't know me."

"Fine. When?"

"Today. This afternoon. Four o'clock."

"Where?"

"That's your job."

"Fine, fine. I'll get it done. According to the press, Amber's MIA right now, which actually works out in our favor, I think."

My only response is to hang up the phone.

I don't want to hear her name.

I don't want to say her name.

How the hell did this happen? I was supposed to wake up this morning in bed with the woman who would be my wife and have my kids, but she's doing that with another man.

I can't even begin to articulate all the ways that's straight fucked up. For the first time in a long time, my fingers aren't itching for a pen to write down lyrics to get this out onto paper.

Instead, there's *nothing.*

Empty.

I pinch the bridge of my nose, and Frisco takes the phone from my hand.

"You really think a press conference is a good idea?"

"What choice do I have? I gotta put it out there, and I'm not doing it through some pansy-ass statement my people release."

"You gonna be able to handle the questions?"

I lower my hand and meet his gaze. "I didn't say shit about answering questions. I'll say my piece and walk."

Frisco's face says what his mouth doesn't. *God help you, I hope you're right.*

I pat the pockets of my jeans and come up empty in the search for my keys.

"Please tell me my 442 is somewhere safe."

As soon as the demand is out, I remember a bright neon sign and that damned parrot.

Where was that? I try to picture the sign in my head.

The Fishbowl.

Zane moves toward the kitchen space in his loft. "Let's eat some greasy bacon and eggs, and then we'll go get your car from Ripley."

My stomach twists at the suggestion, but I know it's the right one. I need to kick this hangover now so I can kick some ass later.

Ripley.

The gorgeous brunette.

Who threatened to bash my head in with a baseball bat.

Great. This is going to be just fucking great.

NINE

Boone

FRISCO PULLS UP BETWEEN THE JAVELIN AND MY 442 behind a run-down brick building. In the daylight, this place looks like it's only a few years from being condemned, but all I care about right now is the fact that my car looks like it's perfectly untouched.

If I hadn't been so wasted and pissed last night, there's no way in hell I would have left her in this neighborhood. Not a frigging chance.

I don't care that she's insured, because this isn't the kind of car you can replace. She's been specially restored by Logan Brantley of Gold Haven, Kentucky, to fit my vision of what badass American muscle looks like.

The peeling paint of the Javelin beside us reminds me of how the Olds looked when I dropped her off myself at his shop.

Before we climb out, Frisco's phone starts ringing for the sixth time since we left his loft.

"I swear, if it's another call for you, I'm going to break

this thing like you did yours."

"I'll get a new phone this afternoon, and you can kick them all to me if they keep bothering you. Sorry about that, man. And thanks for everything this morning. I've toured with some assholes who wouldn't piss on me if I were on fire, so it's a nice change."

Frisco gives me a chin lift. "You changed my life when you asked me to be on that tour, but that's not all. You didn't treat me like shit. You treated me like a friend. So that's what I'm giving back to you, brother."

I extend a hand. "Much appreciated. It won't be our last tour either. Stop out at my place anytime. Tonight you'll find me burning one by the fire, wondering how all this shit happened."

"Sounds like a plan."

I reach for the handle and pause, my mind on the woman I'm hoping is inside with my keys. "What's the deal with this chick? She gonna be a problem?"

Frisco looks toward the weathered building ahead of us. "Ripley?"

"Yeah. The dark-haired one from last night."

"She's good people. Won't let me take her out on a date to save my life, all because of her rule."

He throws up air quotes around the word *rule*, and I vaguely recall a mention of something like that from last night.

"What kind of rule is that? Most groupies can't wait to jump on a famous dick."

Frisco chokes out a laugh. "Rip is about as far from a groupie as I can imagine. I've been trying for a few months and gettin' nowhere. Maybe if I'd met her before the label signed me, I would've had a chance. I don't know. At this point, I'm pretty sure I've been friend-zoned."

"Ouch." I give him a mock wince.

"You win some, you lose some."

"Or your girl marries some stranger in Vegas, and you find out from a skank in a bar." Even though I'm trying to make a joke, it comes out harsher than I intended.

Frisco gives me a rueful look. "You win on that one."

"For all the good it does me."

Frisco waits for me to make my way to the door and pull it open before throwing the Jeep in reverse and gunning the engine to pull out like an asshole. The sound carries inside, and a dark head pops up from behind the bar.

"We're closed," the husky-but-feminine voice calls before she turns to face me with a box clutched to her chest.

In the dim light, she's just as built as I remember from last night—not that it makes a damn bit of difference to me right now.

"Not here to drink. I'll take my keys and be on my way."

When she frowns, I step into the light. Recognition flashes over her face as I leave the shadowed entry.

She cocks a hip. "Too bad. I was hoping you'd forget and leave that gorgeous piece of muscle here long enough for me to consider it abandoned."

"Not a chance."

She sits the box on the bar before coming toward me. "Pity."

"You got those keys?"

"I put 'em in the safe just in case Brandy got any ideas about coming back and trying to take it. Let me go grab them."

Brandy . . . the skank who shook me down for a grand.

Ripley turns toward a door behind the bar as I ask, "She gonna cause problems?"

She pauses, cutting her gaze to me with a thoughtful expression on her face. "Brandy doesn't know how to do anything *but* cause problems. I don't know what she'll do, if you want the truth. I can't control her any more than I can control the weather."

My mood darkens like a thunderstorm rolling in, which is the visual I get from her answer.

"You better hope she doesn't, because I promise you won't like the consequences."

Her posture stiffens, her fingers flexing on the door handle to what I assume is the office with the safe she mentioned.

"Are you threatening me?" Her question comes out more as a challenge.

"I'm telling you the truth. She needs to forget last night ever happened, and we'll be all set."

Ripley's gray eyes match the thunderstorm I pictured as they narrow on me. "If you want to make sure Brandy forgets, you're gonna have to take that up with her. I don't have a damn thing to do with it. And what's more, you don't get to walk into my bar and start throwing down threats like you own the place." She releases her grip and crosses her arms over her chest. "If that was your plan from the beginning, you should've waited until you had your keys first, because I think I've just gone and forgotten the combination to the safe all of a sudden."

Oh no, she fucking wouldn't.

I open my mouth to deliver another warning, but she

talks faster.

"Guess you're gonna have to call a locksmith or a wrecker to help you out. And God forbid if they realize who you are and call the press. You'll be up to your ass in cameras and reporters before you can say, 'I'm sorry for being a dick, Ripley.'"

My temper, already strained to its limit in the last twelve hours, is close to jumping its chain.

"You've got two minutes to have my keys sitting on this bar, or I'll have the cops here."

A cocky smile tugs at her lips.

"And whose phone you gonna call them with? Because yours lost the battle with Hank Williams's face, and I swept up the pieces this morning."

TEN

Ripley

THEY'RE ALL THE SAME. EVERY CELEBRITY I'VE EVER met has that constant streak of entitlement running through them that somehow exempts them from the burden of politeness.

From beneath his ball cap, backward today, the vein in Boone Thrasher's forehead pulses with pissed-off rage. He wants to strangle me right about now. I recognize the signs.

But guess what? I'm not feeling all that charitable toward him either. No one comes into my place and threatens me, especially not after I've called to make sure that his car wouldn't get towed by the wrecker company, even though he parked in a loading zone overnight, and I locked up his keys for safekeeping. Then there's the matter of me barely sleeping because I jolted up at every noise and looked out the window in my bedroom at least a dozen times to make sure his car was safe and sound.

I don't care whether he knows all these details, because only one thing matters. Boone Thrasher does not get to come in here and act like an asshole to me.

I'm waiting for the outburst when he squeezes his eyes shut and balls his hands into fists before stretching his tattooed fingers out again.

When his lids lift, those bright blue eyes clash with mine.

"You ever had your entire life dissected by the media, laid out for the public like your privacy doesn't even matter?"

At his question, my heart lurches in my chest and my mouth goes dry. *He doesn't have a damned clue.*

I shove open the office door and slam it behind me, closing my eyes and leaning on the desk as I haul in a breath.

I know better than anyone what it's like to have your entire life dissected by the media and laid out for the public like your privacy doesn't matter. I also know that they don't care about the collateral damage they cause in getting their story.

But I'm done trading barbs with Boone Thrasher. Now I just want him and his damned car out of here so my life doesn't get sucked into the press again.

I drop to my knees in front of the safe and spin the dial, screwing up the combination twice.

My mom's birthday. Ironically, also the day she was murdered.

The lyrics to Brad Paisley's mocking and oh-so-accurate song "Celebrity" filter into my head.

Boone Thrasher may have lost his shallow girlfriend to someone who could give her more than he could, but at least he didn't see his mother's body lying in a pool of blood on the bathroom floor in the bar where he has to work every day.

On the third try, I get the combination right and yank out the keys with a shaking hand. I rise on unsteady legs, open the door, and stride out—slamming directly into his broad, hard chest.

My first instinct is to jump back like I stepped into a burning house by accident.

Boone snatches the keys from my hand before I can gather myself.

"Thanks," he says, wrapping his fingers around the brass knuckles hanging from them.

"Don't mention it." The words escape my clenched jaw on my next breath.

"I didn't come here to piss you off, Ripley, but it seems I already did, so I'm gonna make myself clear." His gaze holds me in place. "If I hear any reporter or gossip site mention that I was here, you'll be seeing me again and it won't be nearly as pleasant."

"You can take your warnings and shove 'em up your ass, Thrasher. I'm not afraid of you."

He steps back, holding my gaze the entire time. "That's your first mistake. Let's hope it's your only one."

I flip him the double bird, and the asshole has the nerve to laugh at me as he walks out.

In a moment, he's gone, and I'm left all alone in an empty bar with nothing but memories to haunt me.

A squawk comes from the corner. "*Shove it up your ass.*"

Correction—memories, Esteban, and—dammit—that stupid ring.

ELEVEN

Boone

I CRUMPLE THE PAPER IN MY HAND AND TOSS IT ON THE floor beside the lectern. Cameras click and flash in front of me.

"Y'all know me. I'm not the type to read some polite statement from my publicist when I can tell you how it really is."

A few chuckles come from the crowd of reporters, and my publicist covers her face with a hand.

"I'm not an eloquent bastard, so I'll keep it short. Sometimes shit doesn't work out the way you plan. That's life. It's what we do when things don't go our way that defines our character. I'm not gonna run Amber's name through the mud, so if that's what you're here for, you might as well get a head start on leavin'. But I will say this—just because she chose someone else doesn't make him the better man. You want to know more about how I'm feeling? Pick up my next record."

I back away from the lectern and walk out of the room

before they have a chance to start clamoring with their questions.

Once I'm out in the hall, Charity, my publicist, steps forward and announces that the press conference is over. Both Nick's heavier footfalls and the click of her heels follow behind me within moments.

"Were you trying to give me a heart attack when you decided not to read that statement?" Charity's voice is higher pitched than normal, which usually means she's trying not to lose her shit.

I shoot her a look, one eyebrow raised. "Seriously? You actually expected me to read that canned statement? You have met me before, right?"

Nick waves at the door to an empty office and we all step inside as the reporters spill into the hallway. Once he shuts the door, he crosses his arms over his chest. "I think he nailed it. They'll be slavering to get their hands on the next album, which means Boone can dry his eyes about this Amber mess on a nice fat pile of cash."

Again, it's always about the money with Nick. At least I can count on one thing that never changes.

But as for the next album . . . hell, I told them that's where they'd find out what I'm feeling, but the truth is, I don't feel a damned thing right now. I'm totally empty. Devoid of emotion. Maybe it's self-preservation, but I've got nothing to fuel the creative beast. At least, nothing but bruised pride and regret.

My new phone buzzes in my pocket, and I pull it out. *Ma.* She must be watching the news. Nick and Charity are debating something, so I step away and answer.

"Hey, Ma. How's it going?"

"I saw your press conference. Baby boy, I'm sorry you're dealing with this, but you handled it like a champ."

"Just said what I needed to say."

"I know . . . and I know you don't want to hear this, but I think this whole mess is the Lord's way of ensuring you didn't make a mistake that would stick with you for the rest of your life."

I let her words roll around in my brain before I respond. "Since when have you thought me marrying Amber was a mistake?" My folks were reserved when I told them about my plan, but neither of them came out and said it was a bad idea. Now that I think back on it, maybe I should have taken more time to think about their reactions.

"I didn't say it was a mistake. She was a nice girl, but . . ."

"What, Ma? Just tell me."

"Just tell him, woman. You shoulda told him earlier."

My dad's voice comes over the phone, and I picture him standing beside Ma in the kitchen while she calls me.

She pauses for a moment before she drops the bomb. "Amber made it pretty clear that she didn't want kids the last time you brought her around."

The confession hits me like a knife to the chest, because having kids is really fucking important to me. I thought the last time we talked about it, Amber was on the same page, that we both wanted to start a family while we were still young enough to enjoy doing all the shit kids want to do. *Jesus Christ.* How much of what she said was bullshit?

I clear my throat. "She really said that?"

"I'm sorry, Boone. I was hoping you two would work it out if you went through with asking her, but she started rambling about wanting to start acting and how she couldn't ruin her figure with kids."

I clench my teeth as the knife twists. "I gotta go, Ma."

"Boone—"

"I'll talk to you later. Love you both." I hang up without letting her say good-bye.

I'm such a fucking chump.

After I shove my phone back in my pocket, I stalk back to Nick and Charity. "We're done, right?"

They both nod.

"Then I'm getting out of here."

"Try to lay low and let it all blow over," Charity says.

"And write that damned record," Nick adds.

Predictable responses from each of them.

I turn to leave the room, but Charity stops me with a hand on my arm.

"I know you probably don't want to hear this, but it would be a good idea to avoid being seen with any women for a while. I think you can make the most of this by playing up the media's sympathy. If you go out and start banging every girl in sight, they probably won't hold it against you, but it's not going to get you the kind of response we want. Your relationship with Amber really cleaned up that manwhore image you had, so let's try to keep it that way for as long as we can."

When Nick groans, I crane my head to meet her gaze. "Are you seriously telling me what to do with my private life right now?"

Charity lifts her hand and holds it up, palm out. "No, not at all. But I'm telling you that public perception matters. You can screw whoever you want in private, but the paparazzi are going to be watching you close for a while, ready to get the scoop on who Boone Thrasher is going to date next. I'm just saying that we can play this in a way that boosts your career and doesn't tarnish the image you've shined up, so why not do it?"

I know it's Charity's job to look out for me and my image, but right now her instructions are the last thing I want to hear. I don't bother responding as I stride from the room.

Nick follows me out. "The SUV is already waiting to take you home. If you want me to get you some company, just say the word. Charity doesn't need to know shit."

I stop in the middle of the hallway, and Nick almost runs into me. With my voice pitched low, I deliver my reply. "There has never been a time in my life, even before I had enough money to buy and sell you, that I needed help gettin' a woman. You might still think I'm a dumb hick, but I'm a dumb hick who doesn't have a problem gettin' laid. You get me?"

Nick nods. "Sorry, man. I just—"

I shake my head, and he goes silent as I leave.

I love my life. Really, I fucking do, but there are days like today when I wish I could walk away from it all. Trade it for a simple existence where I work eight-to-five with my dad and brother in their small-engine repair shop and coach Little League during the summer. Maybe meet up with buddies at the bar every Friday night for a beer. The life I would have had.

But as I climb into a blacked-out Cadillac Escalade and the driver pulls away through a crowd of flashing cameras waiting on the sidewalk, I think about everything I sacrificed to have this opportunity. The birthdays and holidays with my family I missed because I didn't have money to get home and was too proud to ask for help. Those nights I spent choking on smoke and hoping I'd make enough in tips to eat the next day. The days I spent living in my car because I didn't have a couch at someone's place to crash on. All that would be for nothing if I walked away, and what's more, I know I could never forgive myself for wasting what I've been lucky enough to achieve.

And then I think about that punk kid with more balls than talent who headed to Nashville with nothing but a guitar and a crazy-ass dream.

So what if the media hounds me for every detail of my personal life? He'd tell me to suck it up and who the hell cares, that nothing is sacred when you live your life on a stage for the world to watch.

He'd tell me to give them the best damn show I can, because I worked too hard and gave up too much to do anything else.

Thirty-five minutes later, when we roll up to the gates of my house, I decide that punk kid is right.

I'm Boone Thrasher, and nobody dictates my future but me.

TWELVE

Ripley

IT'S WEDNESDAY AND THE CLOCK ON MY PHONE JUST flipped over to eleven forty-five, which means I've got exactly fifteen minutes before I'm late for lunch with Pop.

My Javelin doesn't like being pushed to her limit, so there's still a chance I'm going to be late, which will no doubt earn some kind of snide comment from him.

Does it make me a terrible daughter that I'm glad I only see him once a week now? When he lived in the apartment above the bar, every day was soaked in bitterness and anger, and too many of them included a stinging cheek from the back of his hand.

I'm not happy he took that tumble down the stairs, broke his leg, and had to spend time in a rehab center. God knows I can barely afford the payments on the medical bills that come every month, but getting him out of my space gave me the buffer I've been needing for a long time.

I pull into the parking lot of the tiny diner where we

always meet. He can walk here from the senior living community where he's living now. Another bill that the "profits" from the bar can barely cover, and my savings account is running dry from making up the difference.

I stare at the diner for a solid thirty seconds before I finally climb out of my car, giving her an extra pat for delivering me safely and not dying on the side of the road somewhere, and head inside.

Pop is already waiting at the same booth he takes every week, a cup of steaming coffee sitting in front of him on the red Formica table.

As soon as I slide onto the yellow bench seat across from him, Lisa, our regular waitress, stops by our table.

"What can I get you, hon?"

"Water, please."

"I'll have the tuna melt on rye," he says to her before he even greets me.

Lisa looks to me. "Regular for you too?"

I glance up at the board where the specials are written. Chicken pot pie. "I'll have the special instead."

With a nod, she swirls away, calling out the order to the kitchen.

"Hey, Pop. How's it goin'?"

His big hands, the ones that never held the seat of my bike as I learned to ride without training wheels, but did teach me how to properly build a pint of Guinness, wrap around the mug.

"It's goin'. My next-door-neighbor's dog won't quit its yapping, so I ain't been sleepin' real well lately."

"Did you talk to the manager about it?"

He gives me a short nod. "Yeah, she says she'll take

care of it, but I don't know when that'll be."

It's on the tip of my tongue to ask him if he's changed his mind about AA, but when he coughs, I catch a whiff of cigarettes and malty beer.

It's always five o'clock somewhere.

"Anything else new?"

He lifts his coffee to his lips and takes a sip before setting it down, and his bloodshot gray eyes meet mine.

"Yeah, Brandy came to see me yesterday. Said you're running the bar into the ground and don't want me to know about it."

That tattletale bitch.

I keep my tone even. "Is that right?"

He nods, his eyebrows drawing together. "You hiding shit from me, Rip?"

I have to tell him something . . .

I knit my fingers together in my lap and squeeze. "Sales have been slow. We haven't had a lot of customers. But I've got some ideas on how to get more people through the door. I've been thinking that if I start an open-mic night, maybe get a few big names in to kick it off, I can really draw a crowd. Maybe even charge a cover."

My dad's expression goes dark and his hand clenches the mug. "Big names? You gonna offer to fuck 'em too?"

The swipe is quick and sharp. I should have expected it, but I wasn't prepared. Especially since it sounded for a half second like he gave a shit about how the bar was doing.

He stares at me as Lisa returns with my water, setting it down on the table with a quick mention that our food will be right up.

I wait until she's gone to bite out a reply. "No."

"Oh yeah? So you mean female big names? You know a lot of those these days? Because Brandy said that the only ones who come sniffing around are looking to get you on your back."

Is there a special word for killing a cousin? Because Brandy is dead.

"Brandy talks a lot of shit, Pop. I wouldn't give a whole lot of weight to her words. She barely shows up for work even when she's scheduled, so it's not like she knows what's happening. I'm the one spending damn near twenty-four hours a day in that building, making sure the take can cover all the bills, including your apartment and your twelve-pack-a-day habit."

"And when it can't? Huh? Where is that money coming from, Rip? Your pocket?"

"Yeah. My savings account. Which is almost drained."

"So, what're you gonna do next? Find some rich guy to start picking up the slack? Because we both know that's what your ma—"

"Stop. Right there. Don't you dare say another word because I will walk out right now and you won't see me again."

I start to slide out of the booth, but my dad calls my bluff.

"Oh yeah? You gonna leave the bar behind too? Because you walk out of here right now, you're gonna kiss that place good-bye. You'd be just like your ma, abandoning the family."

His statement is a slap to the face, momentarily stealing my breath.

I'm the one shedding blood, sweat, and tears to try to

keep the bar going. Pop doesn't lift a damned finger. All the things I want to say scramble up my throat until I nearly choke on them.

Pop knows I won't walk away. Knows that every memory I have of Mama is tied up in that place—whether good, horrible, or otherwise—and I don't know how to let go of the only pieces of her I have left.

I drop back into my seat just in time for Lisa to bring our lunches to the table.

"Is there anything else I can get you?"

The first thought that comes into my brain is *a new life*, but that's not what she means.

"I'm all set, thanks." My polite tone sounds forced, even to me.

"I'll take a Bud. In a can."

And that's a great indicator for how the rest of our lunch is going to go.

Downhill.

THIRTEEN

Ripley

When I leave the diner, I'm praying that my next stop isn't going to be nearly as unpleasant, but part of me already knows that's a naive hope.

Stanley Mullins was the accountant for the bar back when my parents were first able to hire one. Now it's his son, Stan Mullins Jr., who handles the books, but he does it out of the same office his dad did for years. When I pull into the parking lot, I'm already drained from lunch with Pop.

I know that a smart woman would walk away from the bar and start over somewhere else, but I can't. Not just because I don't know how to let go, but because everything I have is tied up in that place.

Nearly every dollar in my savings account has been loaned to cover expenses, I live rent-free upstairs, and I haven't taken a paycheck in long enough to make me question my own sanity.

The bottom line? If I walk away from the Fishbowl, I've got about three hundred dollars to my name and a stack of promissory notes that will never get paid unless I'm there to see it happen.

Stan's receptionist takes me back to his office, rather than a conference room, and my brain is going in too many different directions to realize this may not be a good sign.

Stan rises from behind the desk and holds out a hand. "Hey, Ripley, you look as beautiful as ever."

Being called beautiful always mystifies me because it's such a pointless trait. I didn't do anything to earn my thick brown hair, distinctive gray eyes, or symmetrical features, and they sure haven't done me any good, so I always shrug it off when someone mentions my looks.

I slide my hand into Stan's, and his grip lasts a few seconds longer than normal. That's when anxiety sets in.

"How bad is it, Stan?"

He had a call with a few bankers this morning, one that he asked me to sit out so they could talk numbers plainly.

"You might want to have a seat."

I plop down into a plush leather chair, trying to read the expression on his face. Nothing I see is promising.

"How bad?" I ask again.

"Bad."

"It's just a tiny line of credit. You can't tell me that the building and the business aren't enough collateral for fifty grand."

My accountant clears his throat. "Your dad took out another mortgage on the building earlier this year."

I blink twice as if that's going to help me comprehend what Stan just said. "What? What mortgage? We own that building free and clear."

Stan shakes his head. "No, you don't. And I take it he never bothered to mention that fact to you."

Slouching back in the chair, I lift a hand to my face and pinch the bridge of my nose. "How much?" I whisper.

"A hundred thousand."

My mouth drops open and my hand hits my lap. "You've gotta be joking. What did he use it for? It sure didn't go toward paying off his hospital bills, or any of the bar expenses. He lives in that senior community, which *I* pay for. What else . . ."

A thought dawns on me, one I'm afraid to give credence to by speaking it aloud.

He wouldn't.

"You can't think of anything else he would've used the money for? Booze? Gambling? Drugs?" Stan asks.

I'm not proud, but I answer, "I pay for the booze. As far as I know, he doesn't gamble. He's never done drugs beyond smoking the occasional joint."

"So where would the money go?"

I reply with another question. "Has he at least been making payments on the mortgage?"

Stan's expression turns rueful. "He was. But he stopped two months ago."

When he asked for an extra $500 every month, and I told him I couldn't spare it.

God, the hits keep coming.

"Is it . . . is it already in foreclosure?"

Stan shakes his head. "No, I called the lender this

morning, as soon as I got off the phone with the other bankers, and I did you a favor. I told them your dad has been having some issues and has become more forgetful, and the payments never got mailed. I paid them over the phone, Ripley. You're current now, and they're not going to foreclose as long as you keep writing them a check every month."

"You can't squeeze blood from a turnip, Stan. You've seen the numbers. My budget can't handle another five hundred a month."

Stan leans back in his chair, crossing an ankle over his knee. "I know."

But he doesn't *know* know. I doubt Stan has ever had to worry about where he could find an extra five hundred bucks, not when he slid right into Daddy's profitable accounting firm where the vast majority of clients don't have as much trouble paying their bills as the Fishbowl.

"What am I gonna do?"

"Look, you've got a few options."

At the word *options*, I sit up straighter. "Like what? Because I'm pretty sure I've considered every damn option I could have."

Stan nods and leans forward, resting both elbows on the desk. "Can you get more customers in the door? Is there any way you can increase receipts at all?"

"I'm trying. I wanted to start some new marketing and promo, but that takes money. And when I told Pop I was thinking about asking a few friends to come in and play so I could charge a cover, he about lost his shit."

Stan knows all about my family's dirty laundry, along with the fact that the most traffic I get on a weekend is the gawkers who come with their guidebooks, peek into the bathroom, and leave without buying a single drink.

But how do I keep them out if there's a possibility they'll even spend two dollars on a bottle of water? I'm desperate enough that I can't.

"Look, Ripley, we've known each other a long time, and you know I've always had a thing for you, right?"

I jerk my gaze up to meet Stan's. "What?"

"Come on, Ripley. You know that practically every guy that meets you goes home thinking about what it'd be like to have all that fire in his bed."

The chicken pot pie I had for lunch flips in my stomach.

"Are you trying to make a point here, Stan? Because this is not helping matters."

"All I'm saying is that if you *really* want my help, I'm happy to give it, and I don't think what I want from you would be any hardship on your part."

My mouth drops open for the second time since I stepped foot in the office, but I quickly shut it and spring to my feet.

"I'm going to pretend you didn't just say that."

"Come on, Rip. I'm not trying to be crude, but I did just lay out a grand this morning to save your ass, so I think that buys me a little room to speak my mind. Unless you want to work it off a different way."

I swallow back the bile rising in my throat. Stan's not ugly. No, with his pale blond hair and brown eyes, he's actually attractive in a bland starched-shirt kind of way. That's not what's making me sick.

No, it's the picture of his wife and two kids sitting on

the credenza behind him, and his assumption that he can throw this offer at me because of who I am.

"Go fuck yourself, Stan." Silently I add, *I'm nothing like my mama.*

FOURTEEN

Ripley

"DID YOU KICK HIM IN THE BALLS?" HOPE ASKS as she slides another drink across the bar to me.

When was the last time I was on this side of the equation? Forever ago, is all I can come up with. Which explains why I'm already buzzed after three drinks.

"No. I wasn't going to give him the satisfaction of having any part of me touch any part of him." I swirl the cocktail straw in the glass, mixing the booze and soda. "But I did tell him to go fuck himself."

Hope throws back her head and laughs. "Nice. I bet that wasn't what he was expecting. He comes in here at least once every other week and leaves with his arm around some girl barely old enough to drink."

I jerk my gaze to hers. "Seriously?"

Hope, my best friend since bartending school over a decade ago, runs the bar at the White Horse Saloon, one of the most successful honky-tonks in town. It's always packed with tourists hoping to get a glimpse of a few country stars, and the amount of money and alcohol that flows through here in any given week could probably pay off the mortgage I didn't know Pop had taken out.

"Dead serious. A few months back, he spent all night flirting with one of my new waitresses, hanging around until she was done with her shift. Not more than fifteen minutes after she walked out with him, she comes storming back in, pissed as hell."

I suck down a swig of my Crown and Coke, on the house or I wouldn't be drinking it. "What happened?"

"His MO is to get them into his cherry-red 'Vette and tell them the party doesn't start until his dick gets sucked. Normally, the girls he leaves with are blitzed, so I'm guessing they fall all over themselves to do it. But she was totally sober and told him he could suck his own dick to get the party started."

"Burnnnn." I tip back the glass for another sip. "Why'd she go with him to begin with if she wasn't up for . . . that?"

Hope leans forward on the bar, her boobs threatening to spill from her low-cut shirt, but I avert my eyes.

"Apparently, he had blow and she wanted it. Just not bad enough to blow *him*."

My eyebrows shoot up. "Blow as in . . ."

"Yep. Coke. And not the kind you're drinking."

"But he's an accountant. How does that make any sense?"

Hope straightens and laughs. "Honey, it doesn't matter if he was a priest. Everyone's got a vice."

A tourist in one of those straw cowboy hats hollers from down the bar, while Hope's three other bartenders are hustling drinks and putting on a show tossing bottles here and there. Just the thought of taking a chance of breaking one is enough to make me cringe.

"I gotta sling some more drinks. I'll be back when I can."

Wednesday night is the slowest night of the week for the Fishbowl, which makes it perfect for my one day off. Before my last boyfriend and I broke up, I'd usually stay at his place on Wednesdays, but that ended months ago. He was pissed I couldn't make more time for him, and I thought he was playing a double standard since he was gone every weekend playing drums with different bands, trying to make it big.

Hope used to give me shit about Joey, saying I was bending my anti-celebrity rule, but I disagreed wholeheartedly. Sure, he'd get women hitting on him just like any band member did, but it wasn't because of who he was. It was only because they saw him onstage. It's not like anyone actually knew his name when they saw him play, and certainly no one would ever remember him five minutes after he stepped away from his drum kit.

I've never quite understood the allure of banging a guy in a band. So what if he's in the spotlight for a few sets? Why does that make him any more attractive than a guy in the crowd buying you drinks and having a good time?

"Wow, I didn't expect to see you here. What with you being the anti-fun."

Brandy's smoke-roughened voice cuts into my semi-intoxicated contemplation.

"What are you doing here?" I ask.

Her cackle sets me on edge. I swear, my aunt must have

done drugs or drank while she was pregnant with Brandy, because the girl just isn't right. I want to say it's not her fault, but the nastiness she displays isn't an accident.

"Why do you think?"

She shoots me a look, and it doesn't take a genius to fill in the blanks. I'm sure there are plenty of clueless tourists here to buy her drinks while she feeds them some bullshit story about trying to make it in Nashville. Cue eye roll. Then I remember I'm pissed at her for a specific reason instead of my normal general annoyance.

"Well, Pop's not here to narc to, so clearly that's not it." I reach for my drink and tip the rest of it back.

Brandy glares at me. "He should know what's happening. It isn't my fault his daughter is a complete screwup, running the Fishbowl into the ground."

Her insult stings when it lands, and I desperately want another drink. Thankfully, Hope spots my anxious look and comes down the bar toward us.

"Is there something I can get you, Brandy? Or are you just here to take up space while you wait for some poor bastard to buy you a drink like you do every other time you show up?"

Brandy rolls her eyes. "Give me a shot of 151."

Hope's nose wrinkles, and I have to believe mine does the same.

Brandy scoffs at both of us. "What? If I'm buying, I gotta make it count. It's not like Ripley pays enough for me to buy the good stuff. Guess I should've gotten more money out of—"

My arm swings out and I knock my glass over with enough force that a remaining ice cube flies straight into her cleavage.

"What the hell!" Brandy screeches, attracting an audience to watch her fish the melting ice from between her mostly exposed boobs.

Hope shoots me a questioning look and raises her brows.

"I'll tell you later."

She nods. "Another?"

"Make it a double. And maybe a shot."

An apologetic look settles over her features. Hope knows how much putting up with Brandy stretches my patience. Before she turns to make my drink, she ducks her head close to mine.

"Babe, you know that anytime you want to jump ship and let your pop figure out his own mess, I've got you covered. You could make more in one shift here than you pull down in a week."

"And be homeless?" I don't mention the part about losing my remaining connection to Ma, because in my current mood, I'll end up being the sad sap at the bar with tears falling into my drink.

Hope's answer comes quick, like it's one she thought out in advance. "I've got a futon with your name on it."

Before I can reply, she slides away and down the bar, grabbing bottles and making drinks. It gives me a minute to realize that I have no idea what I did to deserve such a good friend. Apparently, for once in my life, I got lucky. Hope is good people.

"Oh my God, is that really him?" a woman one stool down from me shouts over the music as she climbs onto the cushion, balancing on her knees.

While I'm busy worrying about whether she's going to face-plant on the floor, the atmosphere in the bar changes in an instant. There's only one reason for it—celebrity sighting.

The artist onstage pauses mid-song and yells into the microphone, "Ladies and gentlemen of the White Horse Saloon, please welcome Boone Thrasher to the stage!"

FIFTEEN

Boone

One hour earlier

"That's the worst idea you've ever had," I tell Frisco as I lean back into one of the chairs on my porch, my shotgun resting beside me with an empty shell box on the table. Now that the sun has dropped below the horizon, we're done shooting skeet, and Frisco is talking out of his ass.

"I'm pretty sure that time he wanted to streak through the parking lot in Denver in January was a worse idea," Quarter, my bass guitarist, offers. "He'll never live down those pics of his dick."

"It was cold! Shrinkage, dude. Not fair."

"That's what George said on *Seinfeld* too . . ."

"Shut up, you assholes." Frisco tucks his shotgun back into its case and cracks a beer. "Just hear me out. Nick and Charity told you to lay low, but this whole thing is going to play out on the stage of public opinion. Your fans love you because you don't take shit from anyone. Remember when you called that guy out for shoving that chick in the crowd, and had security yank him? You aren't the kind of guy who goes to ground when shit hits the fan. You come out swinging, showing the world what you're made of, and they worship you for it."

"As much as I want to say he's an idiot, Frisco actually has a point there," Quarter says, popping the top off his beer.

"So you think showing up on Broadway, walking into a bar, and playing a set like I used to is somehow going to make a difference?"

"Not just any bar on Broadway—the White Horse. It's always packed with all those tourists dying to see someone famous. You step onto that stage and mention you've been having a rough week, and then you play your new single and talk about how the girl you thought would be riding in that 442 with you turned out to have different plans, so you're rolling with the curveball life threw you." Frisco's beer sloshes over the lip as he gestures with his hands.

Quarter chuckles low. "Oh man, they'll eat that shit up. You'll have so many pairs of panties on that stage by the time you're done . . . You gotta do it."

I don't give a shit about panties on the stage, or the women throwing them.

Frisco jumps up from his chair. "You're Boone fucking Thrasher. You ain't shy about people knowing you've been knocked down. You show them you're tough as hell every time you get back up, and tell 'em to bring it on. No one takes you down and sends you into hiding, especially not Amber Fleet."

Frisco's words finally penetrate, because he said

exactly what I've been thinking. I don't hole up and lick my wounds. That's not the kind of man I am. I haul my ass up every time it gets kicked, and dare the world to throw another punch.

A rush of determination fills me, something I haven't felt in months.

"You're fucking right that's who I am."

Quarter springs out of his chair. "So we're going?"

"Yeah, we're fucking goin'."

The crowd parts like the Red Sea, and Frisco, Quarter, and I head for the stage at Broadway's famous White Horse Saloon.

The guy onstage, whose set I just cut in on, welcomes me with a huge smile and one hell of an introduction.

"You sure you're cool, man? I don't wanna put you out."

His eyes widen. "Dude, you're my idol. I've been listening to your albums since I was in high school, and now we're standing on the same stage."

The kid's speech makes me feel older than my years, but I know he's not trying to insult me. For him, it's truly an honor to be onstage with me, and I'm not going to take that away from him. God knows I've felt like that plenty of times myself with country legends I'm now lucky enough to call friends.

"What's your name?"

"Theo Sampson."

I hold out my hand and shake his. "Thanks, Theo. You play any of my songs?"

"Every single one."

"Then stick around and we'll play one together."

His entire face pales before excitement lights up his eyes. "You serious?"

"Sure am."

He passes me the mic that's still gripped in the fingers of his left hand. "Awesome. I'll be at the bar. Anytime you're ready."

"Can I borrow your guitar?"

His eyes widen even further. "Dude. Of course."

"Great. Appreciate you, man."

Two of the guys onstage are handing over guitars to Frisco and Quarter, but the drummer stays where he is.

I flip on the mic and speak into it. "Let's give it up for Theo Sampson! He keep you guys entertained?"

The crowd screams.

"That's what I thought. Give him another year and maybe you'll see him on tour with me."

The kid turns around on the way to the bar, and he looks like he might lose his shit. He salutes me and keeps walking . . . right up next to a brunette who looks way too much like the one I haven't been able to stop thinking about. She spins on the stool, her dark hair swinging around her shoulders, and I get a glimpse of her face in the light coming from the bar.

It's her. Ripley.

Coming here all of a sudden seems like it was the hand of fate or some shit like that. Now I know exactly what I'm gonna do. I'm gonna give the girl who can't stand celebrities a hell of a show.

"What's up, Nashville? Who's having a good time tonight?"

The roar of the crowd fills the bar to deafening levels, and I wait for them to quiet down before I speak again. Part of me is second-guessing this, but I know Frisco and Quarter are right. I don't lay low. I face shit head-on.

"I know most of you have heard that I haven't had the best week, and damned if life didn't sucker punch me with that one."

There are a few *awwws*, but I keep going.

"It occurred to me tonight when we were sitting on my back deck shooting skeet that your character ain't forged when things are going your way. It's forged when shit gets ugly, messy, and hard. It's about how you pick yourself up from those cheap shots and keep trucking forward. Ain't it?"

Another roar of approval.

"So instead of keeping the world out of my business, I want to invite you into my shitty week so we can get over it together. Because I bet some of you have had a rough week too."

Beers are raised and more people yell, but my eyes are on the dark-haired woman at the bar, her mouth open just enough to show her shock. *Yeah, sugar, you too.*

"That's what I thought. So, how about we sing some songs and have a good time tonight and forget about all that crap weighing us down, because we're better than that. Tomorrow, the Lord is going to bless us with a new day, and that's something to be thankful for."

The cheers and screams threaten to shake the walls of this place.

"That's what I like to hear!" The buzz of adrenaline filling my veins is stronger than at my last show in front of thirty thousand.

This is what I've been missing. This is who I am.

I turn to Frisco and Quarter. "You ready?"

They both give me a nod, and with a glance at the drummer, we get ready to rock.

SIXTEEN

Ripley

Boone Thrasher's words ricochet in my chest like some kind of fundamental truth as Hope pushes two drinks toward me.

"They're both doubles. I'm gonna be working my tits off until we close, so if you need something, come on back behind the bar and help yourself."

The guitars wail and Boone Thrasher's low, husky growl fills the bar as he begins to sing. If I'd been wearing panties, they would have been a lost cause within moments, but at least I'd keep them on. I see at least a dozen women yanking thongs down their legs from beneath their skirts to throw them at the stage. *Ewwww.*

Within minutes, it's like a tornado blew through Victoria's Secret and dropped its load right in front of Boone Thrasher. A normal occurrence for him, I assume.

How is it possible his voice can be that intoxicatingly sexy? And why did it sound like he was talking directly to me when he said all that stuff a few moments ago?

If I turn back around, will I think he's singing to me too?

Riiiiight, Rip. A shaft of disappointment stabs into me, but I bury it. *It's not like I want him to sing to me. I have my rule for a reason.*

Besides, Boone Thrasher has trouble stamped so plainly on his every feature, a woman would have to be blind not to see it.

I am not blind, I assure myself as I toss back another drink.

Besides, this is what celebrities do. They walk into a bar like they own the place and take it over. No asking permission, and no asking forgiveness. Although, from how fast the booze is flowing with Hope and her bartenders hustling to keep up with people tossing money at them, there's no need to ask for either. Boone Thrasher is probably welcome here anytime he gets the wild idea in his head to step through the door.

The alcohol hits me harder with the double shot, and a plan starts taking shape in my buzzed brain. There's this woman who contacts all the bars and clubs in town and gives them a number to text when there's a celebrity or professional athlete sighting. Then she sends out an alert to thousands of people who subscribe to her service, and the place is mobbed. The tipster gets a hefty fee for it if the sighting turns out to be real, or so I've been told.

I've got her number, but I've never used it. It's not like the Fishbowl is a hotbed of celebrity sightings, but even the handful of times Zane Frisco came to the bar, I never considered it, although I could definitely use the money. Even broke, it seems I've got standards, or maybe because that's just not the kind of person I am. I have to wonder if Brandy knows about it, because she probably would have been the first to call something like that in. *Anything for a dollar*. Maybe it's fate that she's never shown up for work on a day that Frisco has been in.

Even if some other big shot came into the Fishbowl, I don't think I could do it. Scratch that, I *know* I couldn't. It gives me an icky feeling just thinking about it. Besides, the Fishbowl is a black mark on tourist maps.

MURDER SCENE OF COUNTRY MUSIC LEGEND GIL GREEN AND HIS MISTRESS, RHONDA FISCHER. COLD CASE STILL UNSOLVED.

My life would have been totally different if Gil Green had never set foot in our bar. Sadness for what might have been is drowned out by irrational anger directed at stars who wear entitlement like a second skin and take whatever they want, not caring about the broken families they leave in their wake.

I reach for my drink and tip it back. I'm getting shit-faced tonight.

SEVENTEEN

Boone

WITH EVERY SONG THE CROWD SINGS ALONG with me, I shed another layer of my memories of Amber and any plans I might have had for our future. I throw myself into the music, and by the time I'm almost finished with the set, I feel like the man I was before I met her. Before I let myself get sucked into her lies and bullshit.

Frisco was right. This is exactly what I needed tonight. Not just for the gossip rags to pick up and circulate, but for *me.*

"How about one more song?"

Everyone in the bar hollers, and I nod at Frisco and Quarter. They both know what I'm thinking.

"When I wrote this song, I thought I was writing it about a woman I'd already met, but we all know how that turned out. Now I realize I wrote this song about the woman I'll eventually find who'll ride shotgun with me for life."

The chorus of *Me!* and *I want to ride with you!* grows louder and louder until I strum my guitar and we blow the roof off the bar with my latest single.

When Frisco, Quarter, and I step off the stage, security crowds around us and leads us toward the back door.

"Easier to get you out this way, Mr. Thrasher. The crowd's a little wild tonight."

"Fine with me."

"Hold up!" Frisco yells.

"What?"

"I ain't done with tonight. I'm ready to do some real drinking and partying now."

Quarter nods, and the head security guy looks back at me.

"Up to you, man."

These guys have created a wall, but I can still see the hands of fans trying to touch me. I've accomplished what I came here to do, and there's no reason for me to stay.

"I'm straight. You guys can hang around as long as you want." They both reach out and we swap handshakes.

"Catch you later, brother. You slayed it tonight. This is going to be on every gossip site within hours. Boone Thrasher is *back*."

I open my mouth to say that I never left, but Frisco and Quarter are already sliding out from between the security crew and disappearing into the raucous crowd.

"You ready?" one of the guys asks me.

"Yeah, let's move."

We start walking again, this time slower as they cut

through the mass of people. We're about ten feet from the end of the bar when I see her again.

Ripley.

Except she's not alone. She's pinned against the wood by two men, and has a panicked look in her eyes as she struggles to get out from between them.

I grab the shoulder of the guy in front of me. "Hold up! You got a bigger security problem than me, man." He stops as I point at Ripley where she's yelling to a bartender. The woman flipping bottles doesn't catch her distress signal.

"We'll get you out of here first, and then we'll come back to take care of her. She'll be fine for a few minutes."

Ripley flings out both hands and shoves one man a foot back, but he's on her again in less than a second.

"You got your priorities screwed up, man. Women first, every fucking time." I duck between the two men and head for Ripley.

There's nothing that pisses me off more than a man putting his hands on a woman who doesn't want it, and when it comes to this woman, I'm seeing red.

"Hey! Assholes! What the fuck do you think you're doing?" I dodge the grasping fingers of women trying to get to me and lose my hat in the process, but I finally get the attention of the guys trapping Ripley.

"None of your business," the guy in a cowboy hat that looks like he bought it today slurs as Ripley's wild gray eyes meet mine. "Move along."

"You made it my business when she shoved you back and you couldn't take a hint."

"Who the hell do you think you are?"

Without my hat on, I suppose I don't look the same as I did onstage, but before I can tell him exactly who I am, Ripley knees him in the balls.

Triumph fills her face as he goes down, but his hand lashes out and snags her shirt, yanking it down so her tits, spilling over her bra cups, are bared.

I rear back to deliver a blow but security beats me to it, yanking the douchebag away . . . but Ripley's shirt goes with him as his grip tears it down the center.

Her hands go to her chest, trying to cover herself, and I'm more worried about her than dumbass number two.

Mistake.

A fist comes flying out of my peripheral vision and glances off my chin. Another of the security guys dives at the man, taking him down.

"Get her! We're leaving!"

The man who had initially said they'd handle Ripley after they had me clear takes her by the arm and pulls her along.

Something about seeing another man's hands on her after she fended off two dicks who couldn't take no for an answer rubs me the wrong fucking way.

"Let go of her."

His gaze cuts to mine as I reach out and wrap an arm around her shoulders, blocking anyone's view of her bare skin with my body.

We barrel through the crowd to the back door. When they push it open, I'm half expecting the flashing cameras and shouted questions of the paps, but instead it's quiet.

"You got a car around here?" security asks.

I nod, but that's not my main concern. I grab the back

of my T-shirt and strip it off over my head. I hold it out to Ripley, but she stands frozen.

"Take it. Put it on."

Her eyes are fixed on me, but she still doesn't move.

EIGHTEEN

Ripley

MY EARS RING FROM THE NOISE LEVEL OF THE BAR, but Boone Thrasher's words cut through loud and clear.

"Take it. Put it on."

I can't move. I'm stunned and speechless.

Sweet baby Jesus, why is his shirt off?

He shoves the T-shirt at me again, but when I still don't move, Boone Thrasher, country music's bad boy, proceeds to put it on me.

"Arm. Other arm."

My body follows his commands, but I'm dumbstruck. *His body is a work of art.* All hard muscles set off by intricate tattoos.

"Where's your car, Mr. Thrasher?"

"I'm a block over."

"You want us to escort you?"

I think Boone shakes his head, but I'm too busy staring at his pecs and abs. *Good God. Those can't be real.*

"No. We'll attract less attention without you."

"If you're sure."

"I'm sure."

Boone wraps an arm around my shoulders, and I'm so drunk and stunned by his physical perfection that I stumble along beside him. His T-shirt hangs like a dress on me, but it doesn't stop me from climbing into his beautiful car when we reach it.

"Where are we going?" I ask, but he shuts the passenger door without replying. When he slides into the driver's seat, I stare at him with only the glow of the street light illuminating the interior.

"I'm taking you home before you end up raped and God knows what else."

The harsh tone of his voice straightens my spine. "I was fine. I would've handled it."

He reaches over me, his arm brushing my chest as he snags the seat belt and buckles it into place before taking care of his own.

"Sure you were. You were handling yourself right into being the meat in a tourist sandwich whether you wanted it or not."

"You don't know that—"

"You're drunk and you're female. That puts you at a disadvantage. You work in a bar. You should know firsthand what can happen when girls like you go out drinking by themselves. Why would you set yourself up to be a target for assholes like that?"

I narrow my eyes. "I'm sorry, but most of us don't have an entourage to follow us everywhere we go, no matter the time of day. And I wasn't alone. My best friend is the head bartender."

He shakes his head and mumbles something I can't make out.

"Excuse me? I didn't quite catch what you said, Mr. Country Superstar, who can walk into any bar and take the stage and have an entire Victoria's Secret worth of panties get thrown at him."

I know I'm babbling, but I'm too drunk to care. In my head, Boone Thrasher is tied up with everything I hate, and hauling me out of a bar and lecturing me just pisses me off even more, regardless of how amazing he looks shirtless.

Quit thinking about that, Ripley.

"I said you're drunk, and you're lucky I was there." Boone's tone comes out gruff and too much like a reprimand for my taste.

I hold up both hands. "Oh, I'm *lucky*, am I? You don't know shit, jackass."

"I know you're drunk."

"Yeah, well . . . you're the one with no shirt on."

He turns the key and the engine roars to life as he shoots me a look that I don't currently have the vocabulary to describe. "You're really gonna bust my balls for giving you my shirt so you're not walking around topless?"

Memories of the *oh shit* moment when my shirt ripped down the center and plenty of people in the bar got a view of my sheer bra enter my foggy brain. If not for the wall of security around Boone coming to the rescue, my humiliation would burn a whole lot hotter.

"You didn't have to give me your shirt," I say, not coming up with any other kind of argument. "I would've been fine." I glance down as he shakes his head.

Holy crap. I'm wearing Boone Thrasher's shirt. I don't know why it's just occurring to me, but I lift the hem to my nose and sniff.

The scent of clean, woodsy *man* fills my nose. It smells too good for my peace of mind. But still, I take another deep breath. *Yum.*

"What the hell are you doing?"

My head jerks left and I find Boone staring at me. *Oh my God, he just busted me sniffing his shirt. Jesus H. Christ. I'm such a creeper.*

"Nothing. Nothing at all." The words all come out in a single rush of breath. Desperate to change the subject, I watch as he puts the car in gear. "Where are you taking me?"

"Home, where you should've stayed if you were planning to get hammered. Now I just need you to tell me where that is."

His tone, a mix of scolding and condescension, pushes me over the edge, and I decide that I've had *enough*. I can get myself home. I go for the door handle, yank it open, and try to climb out, but the seat belt snaps me back in place.

"What are you doing? Close the damned door."

I fumble to release the buckle but Boone is quicker, reaching across me and wrenching the door shut, then slamming his hand down on the lock.

"I was getting out."

Boone shakes his head. "You're nuts, you know that? You think I'm letting you out here when I wouldn't leave you alone in a bar? Not a chance. If you gotta hurl, let me know. Because if you puke in this car, I'll send you the bill for the cleanup."

I'm gearing up to rip him a new one until he adds the last part about the bill. That threat steals my thunder and instead produces a cackle the likes of which has never left my lips before.

"You think that's funny?" Boone demands, probably thinking I'm batshit crazy, and rightly so.

"What's funny is you think I could pay it. Maybe if I'd sold you out the other night. Maybe then I'd have an extra ten bucks to do a damn thing, but I don't. I respected your privacy. I didn't even hit you up for cash to keep quiet like my cousin did."

The past and the present collide in my head as I continue my rant. "You want to know why I didn't? Because I don't need the Fishbowl famous for another country music legend dying there. Guess you're lucky you made it out alive."

NINETEEN

Boone

RIPLEY'S DRUNK.

Not even drunk. She's blitzed. Hammered. Shit-faced. And she's the cutest frigging drunk I've ever seen, even if she's a little on the crazy side.

Her words about dying stop my thoughts cold.

"Wait, what are you talking about?"

"You. Good thing you didn't go to the bathroom or you could be another dot on the tourist map showing where you died."

That's when it hits me.

I *have* heard of the Fishbowl before. Everyone has. How did I not remember?

Rumor has it that the owner's wife was Gil Green's mistress, and they were screwing in the bathroom when they were both murdered while there was a bar full of people just outside the door. No one heard their cries for help, but the gossips couldn't decide if it was because of the performance going on right then or if they didn't have a chance to scream.

The owner was cleared because he was serving drinks during the murder, and there was no evidence he hired a hit man to kill his cheating wife and her lover. No other suspects were ever seriously questioned because no alternative motive could be identified.

According to gossip, business tanked practically overnight, except for the gawkers. All the little things that Ripley had said the first night I met her, and the next morning when I picked up my car, finally come together to complete the puzzle.

Ripley's mother was murdered in the bar she's fighting to keep afloat. *Jesus fucking Christ.*

Instead of the hundred different thoughts rushing through my brain, I ask, "Do you live above the bar or somewhere else?"

"Above the bar, but I can walk. It's not far."

I ignore her and pull out into traffic. There's no way I'm letting her walk.

"Not happening."

"You're not the boss of me, Boone Thrasher. Let me out of this car!"

She can yell all she wants, but I'm not letting her out until she's somewhere safe. I didn't get her away from those two assholes inside the White Horse to leave her to the predators that could be walking the streets.

It's clear she doesn't think much of me, but that doesn't mean I'm not going to help her anyway. At least now her rule about celebrities makes sense. I wonder why Frisco never put it together? Or maybe he did and never mentioned it to me?

She grabs for the door handle again.

"Hey, settle down. I'll have you there in a minute."

"Don't tell me what to do."

I glance over. In the glow of the streetlights, her dark hair is wild around the stubborn set of her features. I've been out of a relationship for four days, but my dick doesn't care about that as it goes half-hard at her headstrong declaration. *I'll tell you what to do and you'll like it* is my instinctive reaction.

Her contrary nature should piss me off, but instead it's doing the opposite—which ends up pissing me off anyway.

Before Amber, I went through women like I went through towns on my early low-budget tours—one blurry night of fun and forgotten the next morning. But all that changed when I stood in the hospital as my brother walked out of the delivery room holding a little blue bundle up in the air as he called out, "It's a boy."

All those mornings of waking up next to a woman whose name I didn't remember might have fit the stereotype Ripley has pegged me with, but in all other respects, I've never fit that mold. I don't wear a cowboy hat and boots onstage. I don't sing with a heavy twang. I break the rules and forge new ground. I refuse to be a stereotype.

I thought with Amber I'd rid myself of that last remaining trace, but we all know how that worked out.

"Watch out!"

I'm halfway through the intersection when Ripley yells and I look to the right. My foot slams down on the gas and the 442 surges forward, just missing being T-boned by a truck running a red light.

Ripley slaps her hand over her chest. "Oh my God. We

could've died. Right here. Right now."

My heart is hammering from the near miss, and my hands tighten on the wheel before turning us down the side street leading to the Fishbowl. I don't speak until I park behind the building next to Ripley's Javelin. I hope to fuck she didn't walk to the bar, but it's a moot point now.

"Asshole was probably drunk, running a red light like that."

Ripley's eyes are wide, an expression on her face I can't identify. "I almost died."

I reach out and drop a hand on her knee. "You didn't. You're fine."

"It would've all been that asshole Stan's fault."

Now she's talking drunken gibberish because that doesn't make a bit of sense.

"Who the hell is Stan? Was he driving that truck?" I make a mental note to track the guy down and beat his ass if he was.

She shakes her head, bringing a hand up to her temple, and I assume her world is spinning right now.

"No, but it's still his fault. And Brandy and Pop. All of them. I should just walk away from it all. Why do I put myself through this?" Ripley drops her head forward and her dark mane of hair obscures her face. "Why can't I just let go?"

That's when I realize she's not talking about the truck. She's talking about her life. It doesn't take a genius to recognize that things are bad at the Fishbowl. If it was that empty on a Saturday night when Frisco took me there, I can't imagine how dead it must be every other night of the week.

In fact, it looks completely dark inside. The neon light next to the back door is off too.

"You supposed to be open tonight?" I ask.

"No. I mean, we used to be, but Wednesdays are bingo night and Earl and Pearl don't even come in, so it seemed like a waste to just stay open for a random passerby."

The fact that they're not open because the old couple is playing bingo might be the saddest thing I've ever heard, but I'm not about to tell Ripley that.

She tugs at the door handle again and struggles to pull it open.

"Hold on, sugar. I'll get you out."

I turn off the engine and slide out of the car, planning to come around and get her door. She's still fumbling with the old-school buckle when I open the door.

"Here, let me." I brush away her hands and unhook the latch. For the first time since we left the White Horse, I take a second to appreciate her curvy legs tucked into red tooled-leather boots, and the short black skirt peeking out from beneath the hem of my T-shirt.

I try to picture what she was wearing at the bar before her shirt was torn. It was red with a deep vee cut down the front. With that skirt and boots and her curves . . . damn.

I don't mean to say the words out loud, but they come anyway. "I can see why you attracted so much attention tonight."

TWENTY

Ripley

"I can see why you attracted so much *attention tonight.*"

Such a man thing to say, and one that puts me on guard immediately.

"I can wear whatever I want. It doesn't mean it's some sort of invitation to be pawed at."

Boone's big tattooed hands—hands that made incredible sounds tonight with a guitar—pull the seat belt away and I bolt out of the car, stumbling into his naked chest, nearly sending both of us sprawling. His arms wrap around me, pulling me against his blazing-hot body, keeping us both steady and upright.

Oh, sweet Jesus. I'm touching Boone Thrasher's naked chest. I hate that I'm freaking out over this, but I tell myself that it wouldn't matter whose chest it was because *holy crap*, this guy is rock solid.

"Whoa, sugar. I wasn't trying to piss you off, but it seems like I'm damn good at that anyway."

Both of my palms are pressed flat against his skin, and in my drunken state, my tongue is way too loose.

"Jesus, you're built like a beast."

"No more than you're built like a bombshell."

I feel his husky response in all the places I shouldn't. My nipples harden into deceitful little points, and I'm not even going to give credence to what's happening elsewhere in my body.

I want to hate him. Everything about him. He shouldn't make me want to climb him like a mountain to plant a flag at the top saying RIPLEY WAS HERE. *No way. No how.*

But my body doesn't get the memo.

Shoving against his chest, I step back, out of the warm circle of his arms. When I spin toward the door, my legs get tangled up and I stumble forward again.

"Shit, girl. How much did you have to drink?"

"Don't lecture me about drinking. It's not like I haven't watched you do it too."

I try the door, but obviously, it's locked. I jam my hand into my purse and feel around for my keys, but apparently I take too long.

"For the love of God, woman, let me do it or we'll be out here all night."

I snap my head around to glare at him. "You can go anytime."

"Like I'm going to leave you alone in the dark in this neighborhood. I didn't go through all this trouble to get you home in one piece to leave you out here to fend for yourself."

"I'm perfectly capable of taking care of myself. No one has bothered to give a shit about me up to this point, and I turned out just fine."

I don't think about how pathetic my statement is because I'm too worried about digging through my purse. I shake the bag and hear the keys jingle, but for some reason, I can't put my fingers on them.

Boone snatches the purse from me and produces them in a moment. He shoves them one by one in the door until it opens, and follows me inside.

"What are you doing?" I hear the rustle of Esteban in his cage, but he says nothing, so I assume the parrot is too tired to care.

Boone pulls the door shut and it locks behind him.

"Why are you still here?" I keep my voice hushed just in case Esteban isn't completely asleep. My question doesn't come out very friendly, but I cut myself some slack because I'm worried not only about waking up a parrot, but also trying to send my body the message that we don't like Boone Thrasher and my nipples need to calm down.

My body is *still* not getting the memo.

"I'm here to make sure you don't break your neck getting upstairs. Come on, wild thing. Let's put you to bed so I can find mine."

An image of a half-naked Boone Thrasher laying me down on my old blue quilt, pressing his hard, hot body into mine as he makes me forget the complete shitstorm of my life for a few hours, has my mouth watering.

Sweet baby Jesus. I want him.

Stop, Ripley.

Heat burns low in my belly, and I'm terrified of what I might do if I don't toss my ass in a cold shower.

"I'm fine." I spin around and stride toward the light switch.

Except in my drunken state, my coordination isn't nearly as good as it is in my head, and once again, I find myself pressed up against Boone's bare chest.

This is so unfair. How am I supposed to hate him when he smells so good, and I could just open my mouth and take a little lick and find out if he tastes as good as he smells . . .

Oh my God. I need to stop. Now.

But the dark scruff on his chin brushes my cheek as he lowers his head to speak, and I'm caught up again.

"Just let me help you. Consider it my good deed for the day, and I'll get out of your life."

My brain protests that we don't want him to leave because we'd rather climb him. *Why am I using the royal "we"? I really am drunk. Maybe that's why he's being so un-assholish.*

"Why aren't you being an asshole?" The question pops out of my mouth because apparently I decided I needed an answer to it.

Boone's chest—still bare and emanating with a scent that makes my pheromones lose their ever-loving shit—shakes with a burst of laughter. The vibrations ripple down my body, settling between my legs before traveling all the way to the soles of my boots.

He lifts his head. "Sugar, if you could read my mind right now, you'd know it's taking everything I've got not to be an asshole."

I look up and meet those brilliant blue eyes. *How can they be soft and burning at the same time?*

"What do you mean?"

The heat overwhelms the softness, and it flashes through me like the vibrations, centering right on my clit.

A second later, Boone clears his throat, snuffs out the fire, and sets me away from him like I just told him I had a mild case of genital warts. *Which, for the record, I do not have. Mild or otherwise.*

"Your place is upstairs?" His tone turns gruff, and I suddenly feel like the stupid drunk girl who needs to shut her mouth.

"Yeah, but you don't need to go any further. I got this."

Instead of letting me walk away, Boone growls and I find myself upside down, flung over his shoulder as he flips on the light for the back stairway.

"What the hell are you—"

"Saving us both from making a huge mistake. Now, stop moving before I drop your ass."

What mistake? Wait, does he mean . . . The threat of being dropped stills my struggles the rest of the way up the stairs, but my mind spins.

Stop, Rip. Just stop thinking completely.

When we get to the door at the top, Boone grabs the handle at the same moment I tell him, "It's locked. It's the black key."

With a grunt, he palms the keys and jams the black one into the single lock on the door.

"You don't even have a dead bolt. How the hell is that safe?" Inside the apartment, he lowers me to my feet but keeps glaring at the door. "You need a dead bolt. One kick and that door is toast, and you're at the mercy of anyone who breaks in."

More streaks of heat flash through my body at his concern.

When is the last time someone worried about me? Why

is that such a turn-on? Oh my God, I need to get him out of here before I *make a huge mistake.*

I hit the switch, and a dim glow fills the living room and kitchen area. The spare bedroom is on the right, and my room is on the left. My earlier vision of him pressing me into the quilt comes back as my gaze sticks on the hard ridges of his pecs before skipping down his abs.

I have to get him out of here. My anti-celebrity barriers are falling with every indication that he might actually be a decent human being—with a little help from his insane body. I don't care if that makes me shallow, because I don't know any woman who wouldn't drool over that six-pack. Or, wait, *is that an eight-pack?*

In the midst of counting his abs—like an idiot, I might add—I remind myself that he just got dumped by his girlfriend in a spectacularly public fashion. And yet . . . he didn't say a bad word about her in that press conference that I watched along with everyone else in this town.

So what? That doesn't mean he's any different from the rest of them.

Boone turns and I get a view of his back. *Sweet Jesus.* Not. Fair. Those broad shoulders stretched his T-shirt with perfection, and they look even better without it.

He walks toward the door, presumably planning to leave and never come back. This would make the Ripley of an hour ago completely happy, but the Ripley of right now has a panicky feeling in her chest and the distinct impression that she's about to lose her one chance at something amazing.

If I were sober, the idea never would have crossed my mind, but after who knows how much Crown in my Coke and the fact that Boone's body is enough to make anyone lose their good sense, I mumble something.

He stops five feet from the door. "What did you say?"

Oh God, maybe this is a terrible plan. Abort mission.

"Nothing," I reply, the squeak in my voice giving away the total bullshit nature of my answer.

He spins around, takes three big strides, and stops in front of me. With one of those magic hands, he tilts my chin up, forcing me to meet his eyes.

"No, you said something. Tell me."

Why is it that every time he gives me an order, I feel it where I know I shouldn't?

I shake my head. "Nothing."

"No, I'm pretty sure I heard you say the words *revenge fuck* as clear as day."

TWENTY-ONE

Boone

A DARK RED BLUSH STAINS RIPLEY'S CHEEKS WHEN I call her out on what she said.

Her lips are too damned tempting.

"Say it again."

Her gray eyes snap with equal parts heat and embarrassment, and I can't get the image of her riding me out of my head. I was trying to escape this apartment without pinning her to the wall, but she totally screwed up that plan.

Her tone is hesitant when she repeats what she said moments ago. "I asked if you ever got your revenge fuck this week. It only seems fair after . . . everything."

Ripley tries to turn her head away, but I grip her chin between two fingers and get a primal sense of satisfaction when her nostrils flare and her pupils dilate.

She wants me. I know it. She knows it. Now the question is—what are we going to do about it?

"You offering, sugar?" I feel her out with the question,

and her temper surfaces again.

"Don't call me *sugar* just because you don't remember my name."

She's still got me in the same category of every asshole who's come into this bar with a record under his belt.

"I call you sugar because even though you've got that sharp tongue, I expect you'd be sweet as hell once I got you under me."

I'm halfway expecting a knee to the balls like the guy at the White Horse, but I get the tart side of the tongue I just mentioned. "You practice your lines in the mirror, Thrasher?"

"Only the good ones, *Ripley*." I put the emphasis on her name, making damn sure she can't miss it.

She mumbles something under her breath, and then seconds later, pops up on her toes and yanks my head down, smashing our lips together.

It's been a long, long time since a woman kissed me with more passion than skill, and something about it makes my dick go as hard as a steel spike. I bury one hand in her hair, tilting her head to the side for better access.

Ripley moans into my mouth, and I slide my tongue inside to finally get a taste of her.

I was wrong. She's not just sweet, she's spicy too. Her fingers grip my shoulders, pulling herself up to wrap a leg around my hip.

Tearing my mouth away, I stare down at her kiss-swollen lips. "I wouldn't call it a revenge fuck because this ain't got shit to do with anyone but you and me. But if you don't tell me no right now, fucking is exactly what we're gonna do."

My blunt words won't win any poetry contests, but I couldn't care less.

Ripley's response is to tighten her hold on the back of my neck and hop up, circling both legs around me and pushing her skirt up her thighs.

My free hand finds the curve of her sweet ass, cupping and kneading like I was made to touch her. I taste her jaw and her neck as the heat of her pulses against my stomach.

She's going to be as hot as fire, and God help me, but I don't care if we both burn.

The need surging through my veins is primal, and I can't remember the last time I felt it this strongly. Maybe never.

"Bedroom?"

Ripley moans and throws out a hand toward my left. I take one step in that direction, but the couch is closer and way more convenient. I lower us both, and her ass hits the cushion at the same moment my knees hit the floor.

Ripley looks up, her eyes hazy and heated, but so fucking beautiful.

"When's the last time someone made you scream?" I could kick myself for asking the question the second it's out, because I don't want to think about her with anyone else.

"Too long."

Her answer gives me a dark sense of satisfaction as I press her thighs apart.

"Slide that ass out, sugar, because it's time I taste how sweet you really are."

After a moment of hesitation, Ripley follows my directions, scooting her butt to the edge of the couch. I expect to see the fabric of some sexy panties, but instead, all I see is bare, wet pussy.

"Sweet fucking heaven." I breathe out the words like a prayer, wasting no time getting my mouth on her.

The second my lips make contact, Ripley arches her back off the couch, my name a throaty moan echoing in the room.

Possessiveness overwhelms me as I tongue and lick and grind down on her clit until she's writhing beneath me. I want to hear her scream my name. Hell, I want everyone to hear it.

TWENTY-TWO

Ripley

I DON'T CARE THAT I'M THE WORLD'S BIGGEST hypocrite, because an orgasm the likes of which I've never before experienced is barreling down on me. Boone's mouth must be blessed with some kind of country-boy magic, because he's working me over until I can barely hold back a scream.

When he presses one long, thick finger inside and finds my G-spot, I'm gone.

"Boone!"

His name bounces off the walls and ceiling of my apartment.

"Oh my God! Don't stop. Please, don't stop!"

He growls something unintelligible against me, and while I can't make it out, vibrations rip through me and the orgasm intensifies.

I'm not sure how much more I can take, but he shows no sign of slowing.

"Oh God. Oh God. Oh God." I'm an incoherent,

shaking mess moments later when he lifts me into the air.

"Need to fuck you. Sweet Christ, sugar, you go off hotter and harder every time. Sexy as fucking hell."

He carries me into my bedroom, and I don't care that I'm naked from the waist down when he lowers me to the bed.

But I do care when his hand freezes on the button of his jeans.

"What? Why are you stopping? You can't stop." Maybe later I'll want to kick my own ass for how desperate I sound, but right now I don't care.

"Condom. Shit. I don't know if I have one—"

I reach out and flail one arm around until I latch onto the nightstand drawer and yank it open. "In there."

Boone reaches for the lamp switch and flicks it on. A soft light fills the room.

"Don't know if I should be worried or impressed that you've got a box of magnums in there. But then again . . . they're not open, so I'm going with lucky."

He needs the magnums? I send up a quick prayer of thanks and mumble, "Bought them by accident." I stare at his perfect chest for a beat while he unzips his jeans, and my attention drops to the equipment he's packing.

Holy. Hell.

Boone doesn't notice that I've stilled completely as he focuses on tearing open the package and rolling a condom down his tree trunk of a cock.

"It's not fair for a man to be gorgeous, rich, talented, and have a huge cock, is it?" I ask no one in particular.

When Boone's deep laugh booms out, I realize what I just said.

"I guess I got lucky in that too." His blue eyes fix on me. "But I'm about to get luckier."

He spreads my legs and pulls my ass to the edge of the bed before his cock nudges against my opening.

"You still good with this? Last chance to change your mind before I bury the beast inside you and make you scream my name again."

Ummm. Let's stop for a minute and consider—

Fuck it. I nod instead.

"Lemme hear it."

"Yes! For the love of God, fuck me already, Boone!"

He surges forward. I only have a split second to think my words might have been the tiniest bit hasty because he takes my breath away with the first thrust.

"Oh my God. Oh my God."

"It's Boone, sugar. No need to be taking this up with God. Don't want to be struck down before I get to feel you squeeze my cock as you come."

With one hand on either side of me, Boone works his hips, pulling back and pushing forward, each stroke unleashing pure pleasure.

How in the world did she ever walk away from him?

It's the last place my mind should be, but as he drags me toward another orgasm, I can't help but thank the Lord that Amber Fleet is a straight-up idiot.

Lifting my hips, I buck against him, wanting more and *harder*, at the same time knowing I'm going to feel like I got railed by a train in the morning. *This is totally worth it.*

When Boone reaches down and finds my clit, *it is over.*

"Boone!"

My scream turns his name into eight syllables as my

body convulses under him.

His roar fills the room, and he thrusts three more times before going still. Well, everything goes still except for his cock pulsing in my body.

Boone leans forward, his heaving chest pressing against mine as I try to catch my breath. A few moments later, under the heat of his body and with the aftermath of a perfect orgasm washing over my drunken self, my eyes flutter closed and I drift off into sleep.

TWENTY-THREE

Ripley

THE INCESSANT RINGING COMING FROM SOMEWHERE in my apartment wakes me before I'm ready. With one arm, I reach out to smack my nightstand where my cell usually spends the night, but it's MIA.

I roll over, and the bright light streaming in through my craptastic blackout curtains nearly blinds me. My head pounds, my stomach rolls, and I remember why I rarely drink.

Hangovers blow.

Ugh.

The band of my bra digs into my side as I roll again. *Why did I wear my bra to bed anyway?* Carefully, I lever myself off the mattress and take baby steps toward the door to my room, which is wide open.

Since I live alone, it doesn't matter, but on the rare occasion Brandy crashes here, I usually close it. A peek through the doorway of the spare bedroom shows that it's empty, but she obviously hasn't learned how to make a bed yet.

Not surprising.

My purse is on the floor near the inside of the door that leads down to the bar, which I'm thankful I apparently had the presence of mind to lock.

The ringing coming from my purse stops right before I pull my phone out, but starts again a second later.

Hope.

Seeing her name on my screen starts jogging my memory.

White Horse Saloon.

Last night.

Lots of booze.

"Hey, sorry, I was still asleep," I say.

"I was five minutes from having the cops to come break into your place. You scared the hell out of me. I've been calling on and off all freaking night."

Squinting at the clock on the microwave in my tiny galley kitchen, I see it's not even seven thirty.

"It's still early. What's going on?" I head for the cupboard where I keep the Advil, because I doubt the drum line in my head is going to succumb to much else.

"Early? It's late! I didn't want to go to bed until I got an answer from you. I've been up all night. The bar was insane last night after Boone Thrasher left. Zane Frisco stayed and played two more sets of his own shit."

Boone Thrasher.

At his name, the bottle of Advil falls from my hands, the top pops off, and the small brown pills fly everywhere.

"Hey! You okay?"

"Uh. Yeah, sorry. Dropped the Advil."

"You're gonna have to fill me in because when I finally

made it back to your end of the bar, you were gone. Joanie said security hustled you out the back door with Boone Thrasher, and you just disappeared. I didn't get a call or text or anything. What happened?"

My memories of last night are as scattered as the pills on my floor.

"Nothing," I tell her, even though I know it's a lie.

"So you just walked out the back and went your separate ways? I figured you would've read him the riot act for getting you caught up in his shit. I know how you are with those guys."

By *those guys,* she means the celebrity types. Have I always been such a bitch about it? After picking three pills up off the floor, I shove them in my mouth and swallow them dry.

"It wasn't a big deal. It was time for me to go anyway." I make my way through the kitchen around the mess, vowing I'll clean it up when bending over doesn't make me want to hurl, and head back to the bedroom.

What exactly did happen?

The fractured dreams floating around in my head starring Boone are all just dreams, aren't they? I would never . . .

"You sure? I was worried about you, girl."

That's when I see the condom wrappers scattered on my bedroom floor.

Oh. Shit. What did I do?

"Rip?"

I drag my attention back to the phone call, knowing I need to get Hope off the line ASAP or she's going to see through my bullshit in record time.

"Thanks for worrying about me, babe. I don't feel so

great. I gotta go."

"Did you get roofied? Because if you did—"

"No, of course not. Just hung over. I'll call you in a bit, okay?"

I don't wait for a response before lowering my phone and ending the call. I drop to my knees and grab the condom wrappers like they're crumpled dollar bills tossed across the bar.

Maybe it was someone else. Maybe it wasn't Boone Thrasher I spent last night with. Maybe my mind overlaid Boone's face on top of some random one-night stand who was too ugly to remember.

Which would mean I'm apparently now into taking stupid risks with my safety.

One word on the condom wrapper gives my memory a jump-start. *Magnum.*

Boone's voice drawls in my head. *"Don't know if I should be worried or impressed that you've got a box of magnums in there."*

Holy. Freaking. Hell.

I didn't.

I wouldn't.

But the condom wrappers in my hand are irrefutable proof.

I did.

Unbalanced from the realization, I fall backward onto my ass on my bedroom floor and immediately start rationalizing what happened.

It didn't mean anything. It was a mistake. It was a one-time thing. I was drunk. Shit happens.

This doesn't make me like my mama.

I've held on to my no-celebrity rule for so long, the fact that I broke it is too much to grasp in my hung-over state. Then righteous indignation fills me.

I can sleep with whoever I want. I don't have to apologize for it or feel bad about it. It's not like I was cheating on someone—and neither was he.

But what did I do?

Everything's okay. Everything's fine.

Seriously, I'm never drinking again.

I didn't do anything wrong.

It was the alcohol. I was just a stupid, horny drunk girl. Acting my damn age for once instead of twenty years older.

All rationalizations aside, it doesn't matter. I'll never see him again anyway. It's not like I'm getting involved.

TWENTY-FOUR

Boone

IT'S BEEN A LONG TIME SINCE I'VE SNEAKED OUT OF A woman's bed in the early hours of the morning. What surprises me even more was that I didn't want to leave.

Once wasn't enough. Hell, the three rounds we went weren't enough.

Even though I don't know Ripley well, it didn't take a genius to figure out that my presence would not be a welcome one this morning.

Which is why I'm sitting on a rocking chair at the end of my dock, casting into my trout pond at seven thirty in the morning, wearing the T-shirt I stripped off her last night with the spicy citrus scent of Ripley teasing my nose.

There was no point in going back to bed, because I'd reach for her and want more.

How the hell did I get myself into this mess?

Any of the women who threw their panties on the stage last night would have been hard-pressed not to handcuff me to the bed to keep me longer, but I had to set my sights on the one woman in the bar who not only didn't wear panties, but also didn't want anything to do with me. And there's the fact that she probably wouldn't have touched me sober.

Smart, Boone. Real smart.

Now I'm the chump who wants another shot with the chick who probably never wants to remember what happened last night.

I get a bite on my line and tug sharply before reeling it in. The fish fights for a few minutes and then the line goes slack. When I bring it up, there's nothing there.

Probably about the same luck I'd have with Ripley if I tried . . .

But as I cast again and let myself remember how good she felt when she was curled around me, I decide I've got nothing to lose by trying.

I get another bite and devise a plan of attack. What exactly would get that woman to bite?

As I reel in a nice-sized bluegill, an idea hits me. I turn it over in my head a few times, trying to figure out the best way to go about executing it, when my cell phone buzzes in my pocket and the fish spits out the hook.

Dammit.

The only person who ever calls me this early is Ma, but when I pull out my cell, it's definitely not her.

Nick.

"I didn't know you ever got up before nine a.m. What's the occasion?"

"What did you do last night?"

His harsh tone has me stopping the rocking of the chair and planting my feet firmly on the dock.

"You want to try that again, Nick?" My response doesn't leave any question as to how I feel about being spoken to like that.

"I've got an e-mail with a list of links to articles and pictures of you singing at the White Horse Saloon, and then there's some asshole threatening to bring you up on assault charges. You want to tell me what the hell is going on?"

"Assault charges? You've gotta be kidding me. I stepped in between a guy pawing at a woman who didn't want his attention. She kneed him in the balls, but I never touched him."

"Well, apparently he's saying you did."

Now I wish I'd hit that douchebag. "He's full of shit."

"You got a witness who can make a statement to that effect?"

My jaw clenches tight, not just because I know Ripley wouldn't want her name mixed up with mine, but also because the last thing I want is to drag her into a media circus. That would be the fastest way to scare her off for sure.

"If it's necessary. Tell him to go fuck off, or the woman he was groping will press charges."

"Fine. But if it gets ugly—"

"It won't." My answer is resolute, and I hope like hell I'm right.

"Good. Charity's practically doing backflips over the other articles this morning. Public opinion is in your corner. They love the brokenhearted Boone Thrasher, coming out and saying that you gotta get back up and try again when it comes to love."

I scowl, letting the chair rock again. "Pretty sure that's

not what I said."

"Well, that's what the headlines say, so Charity's happy as shit. The first YouTube video posted from last night has over a half million hits already. Bet it'll get to a million by the end of the day."

Jesus, not exactly what I planned when I walked into the White Horse Saloon, but then again, I don't regret it either.

Any of it.

"So why do you sound so pissed off?"

I cast again, not willing to let Nick cost me another fish when I rarely get a chance to drop a line in this early, if ever.

"Amber's camp is starting to make noises, and the better you look, the louder they're getting."

"What kind of noises?"

Nick pauses and his voice drops low, like he's worried about being overheard. "I got word late last night that there's a chance she's filing for an annulment this week."

"An annulment? You've gotta be joking."

"Britney did it. So did Kenny Chesney. So it's not like Amber will be the first. Shit, I bet they already had odds on how long that marriage would last in Vegas."

Even though Amber has only officially been out of my life for less than a week, with every day that passes, I realize the writing has been on the wall for much longer and I was too blind to see it. Or maybe I just didn't want to see it. I haven't seen her in over a month. Even when we were in the same city on the same night, we couldn't manage to connect. Before the proposal, I hadn't heard her voice in ten days. We'd communicated solely through texts.

What kind of relationship is that?

Not much of one, in my opinion.

The more distance I get from her, the more perspective I find. I loved the *idea* of Amber, but now I'm starting to wonder if I ever loved *her*. It's a hell of a realization to chew on as the sun rises on this beautiful Tennessee morning.

"From here on out, feel free to keep anything you hear about Amber to yourself. I closed that chapter and I'm moving on."

"What if she hasn't?" Nick asks.

I sit up straighter. "I think she closed it pretty loud and clear when she married another man."

"Fine, but I'm still watching it like a ticking time bomb."

"That's your job, Nick. Not mine. Anything else I can help you with today?"

"Yeah, call Charity when it's a decent hour. You've got a whole slew of radio station interviews to do with this new single. Have you seen the charts? It's already climbing to the top. You're gonna have another number one on your hands by the weekend. We'll do some morning shows, and if the radio play keeps going, probably a few of those late-night gigs that I know you hate."

It takes everything I have not to swear into the phone. Those late-night TV show hosts are all trying to outdo each other to be the funniest fuck on TV, and all it does is succeed in pissing me off. They love to make us country folk look like idiots to help their ratings.

"I'm not agreeing to shit yet. Have Charity tell me who reaches out, and I'll tell you where and when I'll consider going."

"Every other artist on my client list would kill for these opportunities—"

"Then hand 'em down the line. Because I don't need some slick asshole in New York or LA trying to make me look like a dumb redneck on late-night TV."

"We'll talk about it."

"On my terms."

"Fine. But let me or Charity know the next time you're gonna pop into some local bar and get the crowd fired up. We like to get ahead of this kind of media coverage and make sure you've got enough security."

"That all?"

"Yeah."

"Good." I end the call and stare out at the reflection of the sunrise on the glasslike surface of the pond.

Funny Nick should mention popping into some local bar to get the crowd fired up. I think tomorrow night, that's exactly what I'm going to do.

Maybe I'll even get a parrot fired up too.

TWENTY-FIVE

Ripley

FRIDAY NIGHT AT THE FISHBOWL IS USUALLY A LITTLE bit busier than the other nights of the week, but tonight is nothing like normal.

A few tourists showed up with their guidebooks around five o'clock and peeked into the women's restroom as if expecting the dead bodies of my mother and her lover to still be lying on the floor. That's not the surprising part, though. That happens at least three times a week.

The surprising part came when they took stools at the bar and ordered drinks. With alcohol. The expensive kind.

Okay. Good sign.

Earl and Pearl showed up and took their regular seats around seven, and Esteban woke up from his nap.

"*Old fart. Old fart,*" he crows.

Another regular, Jim, who hasn't missed a Thursday or Friday night in over a decade, crosses to the cage and tosses a handful of bar mix at him.

"Damn bird. You ever gonna learn something new?

You've been talkin' the same old shit for years."

"*Show me the money.*"

I'm assuming Esteban picked that one up during the era of Jerry Maguire, but he breaks it out when someone hassles him about adding to his vocabulary, which I have to admit indicates the bird is probably smarter than most of the people in the bar.

"Fuck off, damn bird."

"*Fuck off. Fuck off,*" Esteban parrots back with alarming accuracy. It's not like that's a new one, though, but the tourists stare at the bird wide-eyed.

"It swears?"

"I hope you're not offended. I'm pretty sure that bird is smarter than I am, but he doesn't seem to understand that his language isn't always fit for polite company."

The woman shakes her head and laughs. "That's one heck of an addition to a bar. The guidebook says it was a gift?"

I nod with a tight-lipped smile. "He sure was, which means we couldn't exactly give him back when he started to stun us with his expansive vocabulary."

The man orders another drink, and I take his money with a genuine smile.

An hour later is when things start to get weird. And by weird, I mean busy. With more paying customers.

A group of twenty-something girls strut in, giggling behind their hands, and take a table near the wall opposite the bar.

"That's the parrot, isn't it?"

"Jordan wants one of those, but I keep telling him that's a deal breaker. I'll move out before he does that."

"*How you doin'?*" Esteban says before fluffing his feathers.

I cross the bar to take their orders because Brandy still hasn't shown up for work, which means I may have to call in a favor and see if Dory can come in tonight. Normally, I only call her if I'm deathly ill and can't manage the bar, or if for some reason I get called away because something happened with Pop, but lucky for me she's always happy to help. Back before times got tough, she worked here six nights a week. Now she babysits her grandkids during the day and seems plenty happy about that.

I step out from behind the bar to make my way over to the full table. "What can I get you, ladies?"

A blonde with perfect beach waves and whiter-than-white teeth answers for the group. "We're having shots! Let's start with Dirty Girl Scouts. Or would you rather have Redheaded Sluts?" She turns to consult the table.

"Redheaded Sluts. I need a *buzz*."

The blonde relays the order to me like I didn't just hear it myself, and adds, "We were going to pregame, but we wanted to get here early and get a table."

I open my mouth to ask her why in the world they thought they needed to get here early to get a table, but the front door swings wide and another group of girls, six this time, comes in and makes a beeline for the other large empty table.

Earl, Pearl, and Jim's heads all turn in unison, confused expressions marking their features.

Me too, guys. Me too.

"*Party time. Party time.*" Esteban is practically bouncing on his perch at all the action.

What in the world is going on?

But I'm too busy to ask because another group of girls arrives and pushes two tables together. I pull out my phone and call Dory, but she doesn't answer. The door opens again and I shoot a desperate text to Carter, another friend of mine who has helped me out before, then hustle to make drinks and deliver them before taking more orders. I've made more girly shots in the last hour than I have in the last year. We don't usually even get bachelorette parties, but it's like Vanderbilt's sorority row threw up in the Fishbowl tonight.

"Do you have a drink called the Fishbowl? I mean, if this were my bar, I totally would. Just think of how cute the pictures would be. All those straws in an actual fishbowl. Totally Instagrammable. You know?" This is from another college-age girl whose ID I had to check twice just to be sure it wasn't fake.

"Sorry, I don't have any fishbowls handy right now, but how about some shots?"

A cheer goes up from the table, and I'm taking orders and making drinks as fast as I can. We're down to three empty tables when Carter walks in the door.

"Thank you, baby Jesus. Dory hasn't replied yet, and I'm dying for some help."

Carter, a skinny twenty-three-year-old who came to make it on Music Row, takes in the packed bar, and his eyes go to the stage platform in the front corner that's been empty since my mom died.

"They're not here yet? This place is about to be even more packed."

"What?" I can barely hear Carter over the voices and

the music that I turned up.

Earl, Pearl, and Jim are looking cranky at their normal seats at the bar, while other customers try to squeeze between them to wave money in my direction.

Carter bursts into action, and I'm slinging drinks and delivering them as fast as I can.

Not fifteen minutes later, it all makes sense when the door opens and the bar patrons burst into cheers.

Oh. No. He. Didn't.

Frisco and two other guys I've never seen walk in, followed by four huge guys dressed in solid black. *Security?*

But they're carrying guitar cases, and one has a hand truck stacked with square black cases . . .

What the hell?

"Hey, Fishbowl! We'll get set up and be ready to rock your world in a few!" Frisco yells as I take three more drink orders and nearly run into Carter.

He lays a hand on my arm and takes in my shocked expression.

"You didn't know?"

"Do I look like I knew?"

"But how?"

I shake my head. I don't have time to talk to him right now. I've got drinks to make, and then Zane Frisco has a hell of a lot of questions to answer.

TWENTY-SIX

Boone

FRISCO SHOULD BE CLOSE TO FINISHING HIS FIRST set when I push open the back door of the Fishbowl.

The place is jammed with screaming girls, and plenty of guys too. Just like I hoped it would be. When I drove around back, one of the guys we sent was working the door, so it appears everything is going according to plan.

Ripley's thick hair is up in a knot on her head, and she's making drinks like a boss. Another bartender is working with her, and I spot a waitress with a tray of cocktails, working the crowd, but it's not the one from the other night.

Frisco's got the whole bar on its feet, and no one notices as I slip inside. Pulling my hat lower, I move toward the stage, keeping my head down. One of the security guys gives me a nod and holds up a hand to get Frisco's attention.

He finishes the song, and as soon as the bar quiets for a

moment, he speaks into the microphone.

"Y'all ready to make some real noise? Because I've got a hell of a surprise for you tonight! My good friend Boone Thrasher decided to join us to play a few. Make the man feel welcome, Fishbowl!"

The stage damn near collapses from the way the crowd is screaming. I pull a set of earplugs out of my pocket and stuff them in my ears before climbing onstage and accepting my guitar from one of the guys.

Frisco steps back from the mic, and I speak into it.

"Y'all having fun tonight?"

The response is even louder than before and unintelligible, but I get the picture. They're having fun.

"Before I get started, I want to thank Miss Ripley Fischer for letting us come take over her bar tonight to show you a good time. Ripley, this one's for you."

I launch into one of my first big hits, "Sexiest Girl I Know," and the crowd goes nuts.

She's gonna kick my ass for this, and damned if I ain't looking forward to it.

TWENTY-SEVEN

Ripley

I FREEZE AS A SONG I'VE HEARD ON THE RADIO AT LEAST a hundred times is dedicated to me and played live in my bar.

Pop is gonna be so pissed. His logic is so twisted and bitter that I'm not sure he'll even be happy about the extra money coming in, given that it's because of two country stars taking the stage he forbade me to use.

But maybe if he doesn't find out . . .

A customer throws another twenty on the bar, and I decide that I don't give the first shit where the money is coming from. I have bills to pay, and cash coming in the door is the only way I'll be able to keep this place from going under. Not to mention, I want to pay back that thousand dollars smug Stan laid out for the mortgage so I can tell him to shove it where the sun don't shine.

So, I'm focusing on the fact that the Fishbowl is making a killing, and not on the ass chewing I'm going to get when Pop finds out I didn't stop Zane Frisco and Boone

Thrasher from taking the stage. *My stubborn old man would shut the doors right now if he were here.* Well, that's not happening tonight. I push the thought out of my mind and send up a quick prayer that we don't run out of liquor. Then I get back to making drinks and taking money.

In only a few hours, we've made more than the Fishbowl would usually pull in during a whole month. Maybe two. Even Earl and Pearl are finally smiling because I told them their drinks were on the house all night. Jim bolted when the crowd got thick, and his stool is now occupied by a redhead with a blonde sitting on her lap.

One less cranky man to worry about, and more room for paying customers.

"This is awesome! Did you see they're charging a cover at the door too?" Carter yells over the music as he grabs four beers and pops the tops. "The Fishbowl is *back*, baby!" He sets the bottles on the counter and grabs me around the waist to pick me up and twirl me in a circle.

The song ends as I slide down Carter's body. Boone's gaze locks on mine as soon as my feet hit the floor.

"How about we light this place up? I got another song you might've heard a time or two. It's called 'I'll Fight for Her.'"

"Ooh, I think someone's jealous," Carter says as Boone launches into a loud and raucous song about not being afraid to beat some guy's ass for touching his woman in a bar.

I shake my head. "No. Not a chance." I hip check him. "Get back to work and sling those drinks!"

He grabs both sides of my face and plants a kiss on me in true flamboyant Carter style. The people at the bar scream and cheer, and Boone's voice deepens another notch to a growl that vibrates through my whole body.

I push away and get back to the customers lined up three deep. *Paying* customers. I do a little dance inside.

There's no way Boone is jealous.

Impossible.

Boone has kept the place rocking for over an hour when Carter signals from the end of the bar.

"What do you need?"

"We got a problem, Rip." He jerks a shoulder toward the front door and a pissed-off-looking man in a rumpled dress shirt standing with his arms crossed over his chest.

"Who—"

"Fire marshal. Says someone called in a complaint that we're over our capacity."

"*Shit.* I'll go talk to him. Don't worry about it."

After I wipe my hands on a towel, I slide out from behind the bar. I have to yell over the music to be heard once I reach him.

"What's the problem, sir?"

"I received a complaint that this business was a fire hazard due to overcapacity tonight, and just by looking, I'd say they're right. But I'm going to let you tell me how many people you've got in here so we can sort this out."

I can barely hear him, and I'm hoping the words I think are coming out of his mouth aren't the ones he's really saying.

A complaint? From who? This neighborhood isn't exactly hopping, with only a few other bars and a tattoo shop on our lower-rent street.

I lead him toward the guy working the door, one of the people who came with Frisco when he first got here.

"We can't be over capacity. Someone's working the door. We've been watching the numbers." Mentally I add, *at least I hope someone has.*

The fire marshal points over the crowd to the back door of the bar as it opens and more people pour inside.

"And what about that door?"

Oh hell.

"Umm, we'll escort some people out. It'll be fine. I'll take care of it personally. We've never had this problem before, and I promise I'll make sure it never happens again."

Two hammered girls stumble toward the front door and their drinks go flying, splattering fruity red liquid all over the fire marshal's white shirt. Previously white, I should say.

"You need to get at least a third of these people out. Right now, or I'm shutting this place down."

No. No. No. Not on the only busy night we've had in years.

"Got it! Give me five minutes, sir. I'll be right back." I give the fire marshal a tight smile.

Shit. Shit. Shit.

I make my way to the security guy and yell to him in order to be heard. "We have to get some people out. Can you help?"

"I can try." Together, we usher people out the door as the fire marshal stands with his arms stiffly crossed over the stained shirt. That's when the fight starts.

I don't know who threw the first punch, but a scuffle

breaks out in front of the stage. The music stops, and Boone points to someone in the crowd.

"Hey, asshole, what the fuck? You're out of here."

The security guard charges into the crowd, which surges in my direction as people try to get out of the range of the dozen or so people throwing punches. Two girls crash into my back, and my face smashes into the fire marshal's shoulder.

"This is another reason why we have capacity limits," he yells. "These people are going to get trampled. You're done. I'm shutting you down. Get them all out."

"Please, don't do that. Let's go outside and talk about it."

He glares at me with a dark scowl but follows me as I push through the crowd to get out the front door. Instead of the quiet street with scattered bar patrons I expect, it's packed with cars and people.

"I'll get them out. There won't be any issues."

"No, I've made my decision. It's a matter of public safety now." He pulls out his phone as people fight to get out the front door.

"Who are you calling?"

Before the fire marshal can respond, a crowd surrounds us from outside, cameras flashing and microphones waving.

"Are you Ripley Fischer? What do you say to the accusations that you were the real reason for Boone Thrasher and Amber Fleet's breakup?"

"Ripley! Did you consider it cheating or just following in your mom's footsteps by becoming the mistress of a country star?"

"How long have you been sleeping with Boone Thrasher?"

Oh my God.

The questions jab into me like blades, each striking all the way to the bone. My stomach twists into knots as it hits my feet.

This isn't happening. This isn't happening. My breathing picks up. *I'm going to hyperventilate.* Maybe I'll pass out. Then I won't have to face them—

"Ripley! Don't you have anything to say for yourself?"

"How big is Boone Thrasher's dick? My readers want to know! Spill, girl!"

The voices are overwhelming, the questions coming from all directions as I stand there, frozen like an idiot deer about to be creamed by a Mack truck.

How is this happening?

"Ma'am, you need to get these people out of here."

I twist around to stare at the fire marshal again, but my ears are ringing from the questions being shouted.

"Did you consider it cheating or just following in your mom's footsteps?"

I keep my back turned, my shoulders hunched, needing to protect myself from the cameras any way I can.

The fire marshal apparently doesn't care that this evening is tipping into nightmare territory. He has some sort of notebook out and is scribbling on the open page.

"I'm citing you for overcapacity, and as soon as I can get back in the building, I'm going through your fire-safety measures. If I find you're missing a single fire extinguisher, you're going to have serious problems."

Reporters continue yelling at me, tossing out more

demands to know about Boone and me and my mom, and I reach down and pinch my thigh to wake myself up.

This can't be real. This is just a bad dream.

The sting from my fingernails tells me it's not. My reality is actually this big of a disaster.

The security guys from inside herd dozens of people out the front door, and the reporters pounce on the fresh meat.

"Does anyone have pictures of Boone and Ripley Fischer together? We'll pay!"

A guy wearing a Vandy shirt stumbles to a drunken halt in front of one reporter. "The bartender chick with the nice rack? I got a video of him dedicating a song to her. I'll sell it to you."

Oh my God.

I have to get out of here.

I shove my way through the people streaming out the door, my gaze drawn to the stage where I last saw Boone.

But it's empty.

He's gone.

And I'm left to clean up the mess.

I'm always left to clean up the mess.

TWENTY-EIGHT

Ripley

THE LAST HOUR PASSED IN A FOG.

When the fire marshal leaves, I shut the front door behind him with a decisive click and throw the lock. Leaning against the nearest table, I dig the heels of my hands into my eyes.

More than anything, I want to sink to the floor, wrap my arms around my knees, and give in to the tears that have been threatening since the first awful question was thrown at me like a Molotov cocktail by those reporters.

How could anyone think I had something to do with Boone and Amber breaking up? I didn't even know him then.

Who would give them that kind of tip? It doesn't make any sense.

I swallow back the lump in my throat and straighten.

The stack of citations the fire marshal left sits on the bar like the pile of crap it is. In addition to overcapacity, he wrote up the Fishbowl for outdated fire extinguishers, failure to test the sprinkler system regularly, and three other violations that sounded made-up to me.

"What a crazy night." Carter picks up a toppled stool before reaching for another.

The bar is a wreck. Two tables, three stools, and six chairs—all broken. There's shattered glass on the floor, along with puddles of spilled drinks, vomit, and what looks like blood from the fight. Cups cover the tables, some tipped over and leaking onto the floor.

Dory, Carter, and I survey the mess with the same daunted look on our faces.

"You guys can go. I'll deal with this."

They both look at me like I'm nuts. And maybe I am, but right now I don't think I can handle making small talk while we clean up this disaster.

"Not a chance. I'll clear those tables and wipe them down. Carter will get the broken furniture out of here, and you can handle the mopping. Let's do this." Dory sounds like a drill sergeant, and they both spring into action.

I stare at the citations for another long moment, flipping through them and tallying the numbers in my head. I don't know how much we made tonight, but these fines are going to eat up most, if not all, of the cash. But first, I need to make sure Carter and Dory get paid. They rallied tonight with the kind of loyalty that's worth more than money.

Another hour passes and Dory and Carter have finished their tasks, leaving me with a hug from each and half the floor to mop.

"Call me if you need me tomorrow. My daughter picks up the kids at five, so I'm around after that," Dory says.

Carter offers his help if it's needed again too, but I can't imagine it will be.

Can I even open tomorrow with these citations?

I wave to both of them, and the sick feeling that's been churning in my stomach intensifies as the question hangs over my head.

It's the weekend, so it's not like I can pay the fines or call the city and ask questions. The only thing I can do is get this place back into shape, and hope that some kind of solution occurs to me tomorrow before we're due to open.

I dunk the mop back in the bucket and squeeze it dry as my brain turns to worst-case-scenario solutions. If the fines take all the money we made tonight, maybe I can close another night a week and work somewhere else to help make ends meet for a while. I bet Hope would give me shifts Tuesday and Wednesday nights at the White Horse . . .

Someone pounds on the locked back door, but I have absolutely no intention of opening it. I'm done with human interaction today. *Done.*

"Ripley, it's me. Open up, sugar."

The deep voice is distinctive enough that there's no question who it is.

Call it irrational if you want, but hearing Boone Thrasher's voice after I've spent the last couple of hours dealing with the mess he walked out on pisses me off enough to stomp to the door and yank it open.

"What are you doing here?"

He leans back on the heels of his trademark biker boots with his hands jammed in his pockets, his eyes searching my face.

"Can I come in?" He looks around like he's expecting

paparazzi to jump out of the bushes and surprise him.

Given what happened earlier, I step aside and let him in before shutting and locking the door again. When I turn around, I catch him scanning the bar before he turns back to me.

"Everyone gone?"

I nod, my anger and frustration threatening to boil over as his posture relaxes.

"I didn't want—"

I don't know what he's going to say, but I can't hold it in any longer.

"What the hell happened tonight? You and Frisco decided you'd put on an impromptu concert and didn't bother to tell me first? I'm assuming you were trying to help, but we weren't prepared. I didn't have servers, enough people to help cover the bar, someone to work both doors so I could, I don't know, *prevent the fire marshal from shutting me down*!" I'm yelling by the time I get to the end of my tirade, and Boone's expression tightens and his shoulders stiffen.

"You're really giving me shit for trying to do something nice? Any bar owner in this town would drop to their knees and beg us to come play. And, yeah, we were here to help. You made a shitload of money tonight, which was the whole point. This place has one foot in the grave, and we thought if you could get some more traffic, maybe you'd have a shot at saving it." By the time he's done, he looks just as pissed off as I probably do.

"Yeah, well, you trying to help me save this place might have killed it even faster. Shit blew up in my face and you just disappeared." I pause to deliver the worst part. "Not to mention now everyone thinks I'm your whore!"

Boone takes a step back, his face morphing into a harsh scowl. "What the fuck are you talking about?"

"Didn't you see the reporters out front before you bolted? Couldn't you hear them yelling at me?"

His brows draw together in confusion. "No. We grabbed the equipment and went out the back."

I rub a hand over my face and tell him most of what they said. I leave out the part about my mom because I can't bring myself to repeat the words.

"What in the ever-loving fuck?" Boone explodes, pacing across the freshly mopped section of the floor. He turns and pins his gaze on me. "Someone you know had to have tipped them off. This shit doesn't happen by accident. Who would've seen us here?"

The air leaves my lungs like I've been sucker punched.

"You're blaming this on me?" My voice echoes off the high ceilings, and my temper snaps. "Get out of my bar."

Boone stalks toward me instead of heading for the door. His black T-shirt stretches over his broad chest and thick arms, and the heat of anger in his gaze has me backing up until my ass bumps the brick wall. Boone keeps coming.

"Get out? Not a fucking chance. I went out of my way to do something nice—twice—for you, not letting you get assaulted in a bar and then coming here tonight, and you're trying to throw me out on my ass? Not happening."

His arrogance tips my temper from pissed off to enraged.

"What? You want some kind of thank-you?"

"It would be nice." His words come out a low growl.

I clench my jaw. "Thank you, oh-so-wonderful Boone Thrasher, for lowering yourself to try to help me. Please, spare me from any more of your favors, because now the media thinks I'm some kind of home-wrecker, and this bar is dying quicker than before!"

Boone presses a hand to the wall beside my face. "Shut up."

My mouth drops open. "What did you just say to me?"

"I said *shut up*."

"How dare you—"

Before I can rip him a new one, Boone's lips crash down on mine.

TWENTY-NINE

Boone

SHE'S FUCKING GORGEOUS WHEN SHE'S PISSED. THE cliché, and song lyrics to accompany it, flash through my brain before being taken over by everything Ripley.

I want her.

I want all that rage burning through her underneath me. On top of me. Wherever the hell I can get her.

Instead of shoving me back like I expect, Ripley curls her fingers into my shirt, digging into my shoulders as her body molds to mine.

With a groan, I reach down and grab a handful of her curvy ass before pulling her leg up to wrap around my waist. I grind into her, my cock straining against my jeans, and the friction kicks up the need for her another notch.

What is it about this woman? Right now, her brain might hate me, but her body sure doesn't.

Ripley releases her grip on my shoulder with one hand to bury her fingers in my hair and tug my head to the other side so she can readjust, taking what she wants from the kiss.

I let her take the lead for a few moments before I pull back and meet her hazy gray gaze.

"You're gonna strip those boots and jeans off, and I'm gonna fuck you on this bar. After I've got you in a better mood, we're gonna figure out how to handle this."

The haze burns off her eyes to be replaced by heat. "Don't tell me what to do."

"Shut up."

Normally, I wouldn't talk to a woman like that, but Ripley pushes all my buttons. What's more, she gives as good as she gets. I wrap my hands around her waist, pick her up, and carry her to the bar. Her fingers clutch my biceps, holding tight when I sit her where I want her.

With a look at her obstinate expression, I have a feeling she's not going to follow my directions too well.

"You don't want to strip? Fine. I'll do it myself."

"Who says I even want you? Maybe once was enough."

"You're full of shit, sugar." With a swift move, I cup her center, feeling the heat even through the denim. "I'd bet my favorite bike on the fact that your tight little pussy is wet."

She lifts off the scarred wood, pressing into my touch, and her gaze narrows on me. "Maybe it's because of someone else."

Oh, fuck no.

"Who? That bartender of yours? Not a chance."

"Maybe it was Frisco."

Irrational jealousy pumps into my blood. I glance down at her nipples puckered against the low-cut *Man in Black* tank she wears. Ducking my head, I close my teeth around one and tug.

Ripley's sharp inhalation tells me what I need to know. I release it when she arches back.

"Frisco ain't here. This is all for me. You can lie all you want, Ripley. I'll still give you what you need, even if you won't admit it."

"Shut up and fuck me."

A grin stretches my lips. "That's exactly what I plan on doing."

I step back, and with two yanks, her boots are on the floor. Ripley lifts her ass and helps me peel the jeans down her legs.

"Jesus. Don't you ever wear panties?" The sight of her slick pussy damn near takes me to my knees.

"Not if I can help it."

I sweep my thumb across the wetness, dipping between her bare lips. "You're soaked, sugar."

"You talk too much, superstar."

Her words act like lighter fluid, sending my need flaring and my plan to shit. Instead of taking my time, I have to be inside her.

"Get my cock out. I need to fuck you."

For the first time, she doesn't snap back with a defiant answer. Her hands go for the buttons of my jeans, tugging them open, and my cock springs free. When Ripley's hand wraps around it, my groan fills the room. I tangle her fingers with mine to stop her from jacking me off right here.

"Not coming until I'm inside you."

Reaching into my back pocket, I pull out the condom I shoved there earlier tonight and tear it open with my teeth. Before I can put it on, she tugs it from my hands and rolls it down my shaft with another squeeze. I step closer to the bar and fit my cock against her entrance.

"Look at me," I demand.

Ripley's gaze collides with mine.

"You're gonna watch me fuck you, and when we're done, you try to lie to me and say you didn't love every minute of it."

THIRTY

Ripley

MY MOUTH DROPS OPEN AT BOONE'S WORDS, AND he leans forward to steal another taste from my lips before burying his cock balls deep on the first stroke. I reach out to brace myself on the cool wood, and before I can adjust to the fullness, he pulls back and thrusts again. Fast and then slow. Fast and then slow. The changing pace lights my body on fire, and I grab the edge of the bar, white-knuckling it for the ride.

As he pounds into me over and over, I hold off my orgasm as long as I can, like I'm proving some kind of point.

"Oh God." I gasp as the climax smashes into me. "Boone. Shit."

"Give it to me. I want to hear it."

At his order, the moan I've been keeping in spills from my lips. "Fuck yes. Fuck yes."

He hammers into me as my body tenses, pleasure rippling through every cell. Finally, Boone's thrusts slow as his cock pulses inside me.

His groan is unintelligible. He lowers his forehead against mine as I haul in breath after breath.

Pounding starts on the door, and we both jerk our attention to the front of the room.

"Oh my God." I scoot back on the wood at the same moment Boone pulls out of me. "You have to get out of here. Now. Go!"

"I haven't even rolled the condom off my dick, and you're—"

I jump down, grab my jeans, and pull them up my legs. Boone ducks behind the bar, I assume disposing of the condom, and I tug on my boots.

"Go!" I motion him toward the back door as he shoves his dick in his pants and buttons them.

"Are you crazy? It's the middle of the goddamned night. I'm not letting you open the door to someone by yourself."

"Then hide."

"No way."

The pounding comes again.

"I lost my wallet!" a voice yells from outside. "Anyone there?"

I rush toward the door, but Boone reaches out to snag my arm and pulls me back.

"You just hauled in a shitload of cash tonight. Did it ever occur to you that someone could be here to rob you?"

"I can hear voices! Open up! I just want my wallet!"

"Stay behind me," Boone orders.

"You can't open the door. He'll see you."

Boone glares at me. "I'd rather you be safe than worry

about some drunk asshole knowing I'm here. Stay behind me."

With a huff, I comply. Boone pulls open the door, and a kid in a Vandy T-shirt falls forward.

"The fuck do you want?" Boone barks at him.

The kid looks up, recognition clear on his face. "Shit, man. This is even better than my wallet." Before either of us can move, the kid lifts his phone and snaps a picture of Boone and me. Together. With my sex hair.

Boone reaches for his phone but the kid is quicker, bolting toward a car waiting at the curb.

"Go! Go!"

With a squeal of tires, it's gone.

Vandy T-shirt. *He's the one who sold the video.*

Boone slams the door shut and turns to me.

"We have a serious problem," I tell him.

Boone strides to the back door with the little asshole's wallet in hand. Someone tossed it behind the bar earlier, the cash missing, of course.

But at least we have his name and address.

"He's going to sell that picture before you can get to him. Guaranteed he already has the contact from selling the video."

Boone pauses at the door. "Which is why I'm going now instead of staying to fuck you a second time like I'd prefer."

I cross my arms over my chest. "That's not happening again. Ever."

His expression turns dark. "Because of your damn

rule? That's bullshit and you know it."

It wasn't bullshit when the press was accusing me of being a whore like my mama.

"I can't do this. I'm not doing this." My tone is resolute.

Boone tilts his head to one side, studying me. "Give me one good reason."

I drop my arms and straighten my shoulders. "I don't have to give you a reason for anything. I'm not going to date you. It's not happening."

Boone pushes off the door and closes the distance until he towers over me. I'm not short at five foot five, but next to his six-foot-plus frame, I feel tiny.

"Who said anything about dating?"

My first instinct is to tell him to leave, but something stops me. Maybe the memory of the best orgasms I've had in months.

"Then what do you want? A rebound?"

He shrugs. "Why not? Who's it gonna hurt?"

"Me! I'm the one the media says is a slut. Oh, and my bar is going to end up closed in about three months if I can't turn it around, notwithstanding all the fines I've racked up."

"You let me worry about that shit. I'll get people here, no more than the legal capacity, and my PR team will deal with the media. All you have to do is—"

I jut out my chin. "Be available to you when and where you want?" I'm joking when I say the words, scoffing at the idea.

Boone's smug smile is anything but a joke. "Exactly."

"Get out," I snap.

Obviously knowing when to retreat, Boone raises his

hands in the air and backs away. “Think about it. I’m gonna go track down this little punk. Frisco has my number. You let me know what you decide.”

THIRTY-ONE

Boone

I don't know what I'm doing with Ripley, but I want to do more of it. Not a relationship, though, given her answer of a solid *hell no* with a side of *no fucking way*.

I'm fresh out of a two-year commitment, and getting into something new is the last thing I should even be thinking about. *Doesn't matter. Not happening.*

I could have debated with Ripley all night. But with that stubborn expression, there was no way I could persuade her that the sky is blue and the grass is green at this point, let alone convince her that my cock needs to find its way into her pussy on a regular basis, regardless of the label we slap on it.

There's the upside of the fact that I like being around her too, at least when she's not bitching me out for something. Shit, even when she's bitching me out, I still like being around her more than most anyone I know. That's the part I should probably be worrying about, but

I'm not tonight.

No, I've got bigger things on my plate. Like the heap of guilt over how our impromptu show ended.

How was I supposed to know that someone would report the bar to the fire marshal and shit would rain down? Venue capacity limits aren't exactly something I have to think about beyond knowing that *sold out* means more money in the bank for me.

But getting the Fishbowl shut down and Ripley saddled with all those fines? *Shit.* I'm getting Nick on it. He's already texted me four times and left me three voice mails tonight that I've ignored, and after what Ripley said about the press, it doesn't take a mental giant to figure out why. Charity hasn't called, which could go either way. Hopefully, it means she's working her PR magic.

With the phone on speaker, I call Nick as I turn in the direction of the Vanderbilt campus. According to the ID in the wallet and Google, that kid lives close to it.

Nick answers on the first ring, but not with a greeting. "What the fuck did you do?"

"You tell me what they're saying I did, and we'll go from there."

"What part of *lay low* do you not understand? This is a disaster."

"I did a show at a bar. Big deal."

"I don't give a shit about the show. I give a shit about the fact that the media is jumping on the *Boone Thrasher is a manwhore* wagon and accusing you of cheating on Amber. Why would you give her people an opportunity to spin that? All you had to do was be discreet if you couldn't keep your dick in your pants."

I make a left onto the correct street and slow down to check out the house numbers.

"Listen up, Nick. You want to talk to me like I'm a kid you're taking to task, you're gonna lose your biggest client. So, watch yourself. Your job is to handle shit, so handle it."

"Could you at least have picked someone who wasn't the daughter of Nashville's most notorious home-wrecker?"

The comment about Ripley's mom pisses me off.

"Don't fucking talk about her like that."

Nick's groan fills the car. "You actually *like* the girl? Jesus Christ, Boone. What did I do to deserve this?"

"Stop whining like a little bitch and do your job. Whatever they're saying about me cheating on Amber is bullshit. I didn't even meet Ripley until *after* Amber's impromptu wedding, so you can shove the truth down their throats."

The other end of the line is silent for a long moment.

"What do you want me to do, Boone? Have Charity spin this as some sort of love-at-first-sight shit?"

I choke on the suggestion. "How about spinning it as two consenting adults doing something that's no one's goddamned business?"

Nick laughs, but there's no trace of humor in it. "We both know that won't work. If we want to get the press to drop this, we have to give them something bigger."

"Like what?"

I spot the house number on the license and pull off to park on the side of the street behind a new Camaro. *Shit.* It's a frigging frat house.

"I don't know. I'm working on it," Nick says, and I can hear him clicking on his computer keys.

"You do your shit. I'm off to go kick some college kid's ass if he's already sold a picture of me and Ripley to the tabloids."

"Are you fucking kidding me?" Nick's voice turns into a yell.

"Sorry, man. Promised the lady I'd defend her honor."

"Boone—"

I hang up on him and silence my phone as he calls back. I shove open the car door and climb out, jamming my phone into my pocket.

Why does it have to be a damned frat house?

Screw it. I stalk through the front yard and up to the porch.

College wasn't something I did. Couldn't have afforded it, even if I'd wanted to. My folks didn't have the money, and I wasn't about to drown myself in debt when all I ever wanted to do was write songs and perform them. These kids would probably shit themselves if they had to sleep in their cars or hustle tips to eat.

Which is why they'll never understand that hard work pays off in a big way.

When I make it to the door, I raise my hand to knock, but it swings open before I make contact and a guy steps out.

"Whoa, dude. You here for the party?"

Now that the door is open, I can hear music pulsing from the house, but it sounds like it's coming from the basement.

"What the fuck kind of party is this?"

He points to his white shirt covered with what looks like highlighter. "Glow party. Basement."

Great. So now I'm supposed to find that kid in the middle of some black-light rave.

The guy who opened the door turns to leave, but I grab him by the arm and pull the ID out of my pocket. Holding it up, I ask, "You know this kid? He down there?"

He squints, looking closer before shaking his head. "I don't think he's in there. He showed up late and left with a bunch of girls from Chi Omega. He's banging one of their pledges."

"Where did they go?"

He shrugs. "I don't know, man. Maybe back to their house." He tilts his head. "You know, you look like that Boone Thrasher guy."

"I get that a lot. Where's the sorority house?"

He gives me directions that I hope, considering his fucked-up state, are remotely helpful.

When I stalk down the sidewalk to my car, he calls out and I pause.

"You are that Boone Thrasher guy! I saw the car online. Holy shit, man."

I just shake my head. There's not shit I can do about it now, and with any luck at all, he won't remember me in the morning.

I climb in my car and head for the sorority house.

THIRTY-TWO

Ripley

"WHAT IS THIS SHIT?"

My dad's voice jolts me out of sleep as my door bangs open the next morning. I bolt up in bed, clutching the sheet to my pounding heart.

"What?"

He shakes the paper in his hand so I can't make anything out on the flapping newsprint. "I told you that none of those celebrity assholes were setting foot in this bar, and you did it anyway."

Caught off guard, the only argument I can offer is the first one that comes to mind. "Why? What do you care? You never come here. You should be happy money was coming in last night instead of nothing, like a normal Friday night! You're the one who used the bar as collateral, and now I have to find a way to pay off a hundred grand that I don't have so we don't lose everything!"

My dad jerks back. "Who told you about the loan?"

"The freaking accountant, after he got off the phone with the lenders. I was trying to get a line of credit to keep this place afloat while I figure something out."

"You're going behind my back now? Fucking some guy like your whore mother, and you're trying to get money out of this place when it's not even yours," he yells. "I should've let the bar close years ago."

I'm still smarting from his comment about my mama, but I recover quickly. I have no choice. "Why didn't you?"

He glares at me. "I don't owe you an explanation for shit, but this is where it happened. Until I know who put her in the ground, I'm not gonna rest."

Realization strikes with the subtlety of a hit and run. "That's what the loan was for, wasn't it? I give you enough money to drink yourself into the grave, but not enough to pay a private investigator."

"So what if it was? You should want to know too."

I throw my hands in the air. "Of course I want to know. She was my mother!" We stare at each other for a full minute before I ask, "What do you think you're going to do when you find out? Get some kind of revenge?"

"You leave that to me." He tosses the paper onto the bed, and I grab it.

It's a tabloid. The front page is a still shot from the video that Vandy kid sold of Boone onstage. *Not the one of us together.* Beside Boone is a picture of Amber Fleet, her eyes downcast and still looking way too gorgeous.

THE TRUTH ABOUT THE BREAKUP—
BOONE BANGS BARMAID

"This is total bullshit." I scan through the article. It paints me as a home-wrecker, drawing comparisons to my mother and Gil Green twenty years ago.

The sick feeling that never completely left my stomach last night is back in full force. I glance up to see Pop staring down at me like I'm a stranger rather than his only child.

"Who gave this to you?" I don't know why I bother to ask. I already know. "Brandy, right?"

"I'd be in the dark if she didn't. You don't tell me a goddamned thing."

I meet his gaze, gray like mine but dark and full of fury. "No, I just keep your bills paid and your beer stocked. You've never asked questions before, so maybe you should quit asking them now."

His eyes narrow and his face twists with rage as his fingers clench by his side. For a second, I wonder if he's going to graduate from backhanding to a closed-fist punch. The anger stamped on his features says he'd like nothing more than to hit me, but something holds him back.

"Ungrateful little bitch. When's the last time you thanked me for making sure you have a job or a place to live? You want to be jobless and homeless? I can make that happen."

I refuse to cower. Holding the sheet to my chest, I glare at him with years of resentment and disgust.

"Do it. I dare you. You'll be out on the street right behind me because no one's gonna pay your bills when I stop."

"Brandy could run this bar." He sneers, going for the low blow. "In fact, I bet she'd do a better job than you."

I snap back in bed, feeling the force of those words

more than I ever felt the back of his hand.

Tears of rage burn behind my eyes, but I won't let a single one fall in front of him. I'm done with this shit. Done being his punching bag. Done working myself into the ground without a single shred of gratitude for everything I've sacrificed in the name of family loyalty.

It's time for me to stand up for myself for once and prove my backbone hasn't disappeared from my body. It's the only choice I have left.

"Then she can start today. I quit."

Pop's face takes on a mottled red shade as wrath and alcoholism collide.

"You can't quit because you're fired! I want your shit out of here by noon. Leave the keys on the bar. I'm done with you. You're as dead to me as your whore of a mother."

He turns and stomps out of the room, leaving me sitting up in bed, frozen in place, a lump in my throat choking off my air supply.

When the door to the apartment slams and his footsteps thud unevenly down the stairs, I finally move, but only to blink as the tears come, along with gut-wrenching sobs.

What did I just do? And what am I going to do now?

Four hundred forty-seven dollars and thirty-seven cents. That's how much money I have to my name. My jobless, homeless name.

It would have been three hundred forty-seven dollars and thirty-seven cents, but I remembered the emergency Ben Franklin I folded up in my wallet what seemed like a million years ago and haven't touched under any circumstances. Now it has been painstakingly flattened and makes up almost a quarter of my life savings.

Ten years of hard work, and this is what I have to show for it. When I think of every dollar of my own I used . . .

I shake my head. It's water under the bridge. I can't get any of it back now.

The final burn? I didn't even get a chance to pay myself anything from last night's take—which is gone from the safe, even though the stack of citations still sits on the scarred wood surface that has been a part of my life for so long.

I feed and water Esteban while he preens on his perch, hoping like hell Brandy and Pop will take care of him. Somehow, I can't picture Brandy changing the newspaper at the bottom of his cage on a daily basis. And what about his bird treats? They might be few and far between, but he appreciates them all the same. I ruffle his feathers one last time.

"If I could take you with me right now, I would. But it's not like I can stuff your cage in my car."

"*You're fired!*"

Another tear rolls down my cheek. "I'm so sorry, buddy. I'll come back for you. I swear it."

"*You're fired!*" he repeats as I shut the cage door and lock it.

If anything happens to that bird, heads will roll.

Shoving the back door open with my hip, I cart the last sad load of my stuff out to my car.

"Looks like it might be you and me for a while," I tell my Javelin as I stuff a duffel bag with the rest of my clothes inside. "Please don't let me down. I'm not sure I could handle it."

The old AMC's engine fires up roughly, but at least it's running.

As I drive away from the Fishbowl, my chest feels like it's crumpling under the pressure.

I failed.

Somewhere along the line, keeping the Fishbowl open became the same as keeping my mama's memory alive, regardless of how tarnished it was.

But I failed.

The harsh truth drags another tear from my eye.

I drive in the direction of Hope's apartment building, praying that she's there. Honestly, I have nowhere else to go.

I'm so stupid. I should have had a backup plan. Never in my wildest imaginings did I ever think I'd be leaving the Fishbowl. I've never lived anywhere else. I don't *know* anything else.

The sky opens with a rumble of thunder, and buckets of rain pour down.

Isn't this just the cherry on top of a shit sundae? My Javelin's wiper blades work only sporadically, and today just isn't my day. Squinting through the windshield, I pull up to a stoplight and look over at the car next to me.

It's a minivan. A man is driving, and a little boy presses his face against the window and points at my car. The dad turns and gives me a nod, and then says something to the little boy, who peels his cheek off the glass before the light changes and they pull forward.

Arkansas plates. Probably tourists coming to enjoy the

city on a family vacation.

I wonder what that would have been like.

A family who went places together. Spent time together. Outside of a bar.

I'll never know. It's not in the cards for me. Never has been.

I press down on the gas pedal and my car lurches forward, only for the resistance on the pedal to go slack a quarter mile from Hope's place. I coast to the side of the road.

"You can't do this to me! Not now." I slap my hands on the steering wheel before apologizing like my car truly does have feelings. "I'm sorry. I didn't mean to yell. Just a little further." I look down at the instrument cluster . . . and the fuel gauge rests on empty.

With a sinking feeling in my stomach, I drop my forehead to the steering wheel. *This day officially can't get any worse.*

THIRTY-THREE

Boone

"DID YOU SET OUT TO DO THE OPPOSITE OF everything I told you? Because now I've got some college kid's dad calling and threatening to sue for millions for emotional distress because you scared the ever-loving piss out of his son!"

Nick is on a roll.

I've been avoiding his calls, so he finally came out to the house and my security guy let him in. He's on the approved list—for now. If he keeps talking to me like I'm ten, he won't be for long.

Still, I can't help but laugh over what happened last night.

"The kid pissed himself in front of a house full of sorority girls. How is it my fault his dad raised a complete pansy-ass punk who waded into shit deeper than he could swim through?"

Nick's face turns a deeper shade of red at my chuckle. "I swear to God—"

"Have you heard the side of the witnesses, because there were about fifteen girls there who will tell you that I didn't raise my voice or touch the kid. Then I signed autographs for half an hour and took pictures with them while he deleted the picture from his phone and removed it from the cloud. I told him I'd come back for a way less pleasant visit if I found out he was full of shit, and the girls all swore he'd never get laid again if he sold it." I paused. "Actually, I doubt that kid is gettin' laid again regardless after pissing himself in front of that group. Those girls are ruthless."

"What the hell did you give them? Money?"

I shake my head. "Nah, I gave them all Charity's number. They're getting tickets to whatever show they want."

"This better not go to court; that's all I can say." Nick grips his forehead with his thumb and index finger, highlighting his receding hairline.

"Why would it? I didn't do shit. Tell that kid's dad that his son will be in community college if they try anything, because I'll drain him dry for invasion of privacy or some shit. Make it up if you have to. There's gotta be something. You've got my lawyer's number. Deal with it."

Nick finally looks at me again, the color of his face returning to normal. "Can you please just try to lay low? We've got a media shitstorm that's accusing you of cheating on Amber, Amber's people are calling with their own accusations, and on top of that, I need you at two radio stations tomorrow morning to promo that single, which is what we actually need people talking about."

"I thought there was no such thing as bad publicity. And the single is hauling ass up the chart, so you can't tell me that any of this is killing my numbers, Nick."

He looks at the ceiling, probably trying to find some patience, but he's gotta know I'm right. This ain't my first rodeo.

"You're walking a fine line between celebrity and infamy. Watch your step."

"I'm not even gonna pretend to know what that means, but I'll tell you this—everything the press is saying about me cheating on Amber is bullshit. That's gotta be defamation or libel or whatever, because there's not a single lick of truth to it. So why don't you go rattle some cages and see if you can't shut them up?"

With a sigh, Nick stands. "Fine, but you need to stay away from that girl from the bar. There's nothing but trouble there."

The fact that Nick thinks he can tell me what to do always pisses me off, and today is no exception. "Not happening. You do your job, get Charity bustin' some ass doin' hers, and I'll handle my own shit the way I see fit."

He shakes his head and I follow him to the door.

"I hope you know what you're doing—"

"Don't I always?"

Once the door closes behind him, I spend the rest of my day with my guitar, a notebook, and a pencil, putting down more lyrics than I have in months.

Ripley is one hell of a muse, and every time I think of her, I catch myself smiling.

I finally put away my notebook as the sun goes down, and take my phone off silent. I've got five missed calls from Nick, but I ignore them. Frisco's call is the only one I return.

"What's up, man?"

"You might want to google yourself."

THIRTY-FOUR

Ripley

"I CAN'T TELL YOU HOW MUCH I APPRECIATE THIS. Seriously, I owe you," I tell Hope as I hop up in her pickup truck and we head for the White Horse Saloon.

She shoots me a sidelong look from across the cab. "You act like I didn't offer you both my futon and a job the last time I saw you."

"Yeah, but now I'm notorious."

"Stop it. You're still my best friend. I don't care if you tell me you're a mutant working for the X-Men, the futon and the job are yours."

I laugh at her comic-book reference before considering another hurdle. "Will your boss be pissed that you hired me?"

"My boss doesn't give a shit about anything but the receipts from every night. As long as we're selling booze, he's happy. He doesn't care who's slinging it as long as they're not skimming off the till. That'll get someone fired in a night."

When she mentions employee theft, I finally tell her something I've been keeping to myself for way too long. "Brandy's been skimming from the Fishbowl during every shift for the last year and a half, maybe longer."

Hope stops at a red light, her mouth open in shock. "And you didn't fire that skanky bitch? Why not?"

"Pop wouldn't let me. He said I must not have been paying her enough."

"Are you shitting me?" Hope's voice rises an octave.

"Nope."

She shakes her head. "Meanwhile, you didn't take a paycheck for weeks at a time."

I nod because we both know that's a fact.

"I think I'm going to be sick. If that little ho shows up anywhere near me, she'll walk away with two black eyes and a broken nose."

"She's not worth it."

"Maybe not, but she still deserves it. She's gonna run that bar into the ground. I give it a week or two, tops."

My heart pangs at the thought, but there's nothing I can do now. "If she makes it a month, I'll be shocked. Then again, maybe we'll both be wrong, and she'll turn it into some slutty topless place and haul in more money than I ever did."

Hope shakes her head. "She'd have to get approval for partial nudity, and we both know she's not smart enough to do that."

"I'm pretty sure she wouldn't bother with approval before she whipped her tits out."

Hope laughs, but the sound is rife with bitterness. "I

really hate that girl."

I have my own feelings about Brandy, but I can't say I hate her completely. She's one of the few family members I have left.

"Enough about her and the Fishbowl. Tell me what else I need to know for tonight."

Hope launches into an explanation of a few things that I wouldn't have realized offhand, even though I've been running a bar for years. The White Horse is a way bigger, more sophisticated operation, so it doesn't surprise me that they do some things differently.

"You'll be fine. I'll get you set up with a uniform tank when we get there, and you'll be raking in the tips in no time."

I force a smile onto my face. This is my life now. Couch surfing with friends, and everything I own in my car.

Go, me.

"Oh shit, did I get you? Didn't mean to spill that. Totally my fault," the man says, his words slurring.

With a sleeve of plastic cups in each hand that I'd just retrieved from the stockroom, I look down at my white tank top with the White Horse Saloon logo on the front. It's soaked through with what smells like someone's gin and tonic, and now my headlights are on high beams from the unexpected dousing of a cold drink. At times like this, I wish I wore padded bras.

Yay. Flashing my nipples the first night on the job. Employee-of-the-month material right here.

With gritted teeth, I smile at the clearly intoxicated

stranger who has a dumb grin on his face. "No worries. Have a good night, sir." Skirting around him, I head toward Hope to hand off the cups and ask her if I can get another tank top.

"Ripley, is that you?"

I look up and almost run into Law, my ex who lasted longer than any of the others.

Jeez. Just when I think this day can't get any worse . . .

My cheeks hurt from all the fake smiles I've plastered on my face today, and the one stretching my lips now is just as phony as all the others.

Lawrence Diller was still a law student when we broke up two years ago after he kept accusing me of choosing the Fishbowl over him. At that point, I was working six nights a week, and our schedules never seemed to mesh when it was convenient for either of us. Also, he didn't particularly like bars, which is probably why I haven't seen him since. *So, why now?*

"Hey, Law," I drawl. "What are you doing here? This isn't really your scene."

He's wearing a pressed collared shirt still tucked into dress pants, with an expensive-looking watch wrapped around his wrist.

"Just passed the bar exam, so we're out to celebrate." He waves at a group of five guys behind him. "Some of the other associates are from out of town, so we figured we'd barhop down Broadway tonight. You work here now?" He stares pointedly at my protruding nipples, and presumably the logo on my shirt.

Another fake-as-shit smile on my face, I answer with an upbeat tone. "Yep, decided on a change of scenery."

"I thought you'd never leave the Fishbowl and your old man, no matter how bad they dragged you down with them."

His astute observation stabs me through the heart.

"Well, things change," I say through clenched teeth.

"New girl! I need those cups!" Hope's assistant manager, Brian, yells from the pass-through, saving me from this awkward conversation.

"I gotta go. Have a good time. Congrats."

I turn to head his way, but Law catches me around the waist in an overly familiar gesture that would have been fine when we were dating, but now, I stiffen.

"We should talk. Things are going really great for me. They started me at a hundred fifty grand a year, and I've got a sweet condo downtown. I broke up with the girl I was dating for a couple months because she wanted her MRS more than a law degree at graduation. And damn, Rip, I miss you. I shouldn't have walked away."

All his declarations hit below the belt. It's a struggle to keep the smile intact, but I manage somehow.

"I'm glad things are going well for you, but I really gotta get back to work. Um, maybe we can talk later," I say in a cheerful tone that's total crap. My suggestion is completely insincere, but I hope he doesn't realize that. "Enjoy tonight!"

When Law releases me, I hurry behind the bar. Hope's eyes are huge, and she takes the cups and tosses them to Brian.

"Was that Law? What happened to your shirt? What did he want?"

"Yes, and some asshole spilled on me. I don't know

what he wants."

Hope raises an eyebrow as she glances over my shoulder. "He wants one thing, girl, and that's you. His eyes are glued to your ass."

I roll my eyes. Of course they are. Law loved my ass. The sex hadn't been off-the-charts amazing . . . unlike with someone else whose name I refuse to mention, but it hadn't been bad either. Just average, I guess.

"Can I beg you for another tank? I'll pay for it out of my tips."

Hope scoffs. "You get five. I'll get you one if you want to run down to the basement and grab another keg. It's going to get your shirt filthy anyway. I made Brian bring up the last three, and he's apparently on his period now and told me it's someone else's turn." She shoots a sharp glance toward the assistant manager.

"No problem. Where am I going?"

She gives me directions, along with the key to the storage room, and I make my way through the crowd again toward the stairs. I've been hauling kegs for as long as I've been able to lift them, so it's not a big request.

But of course, because today can't get any shittier, Law follows me down into the basement.

"Rip, babe, I mean it. I want to talk. You're the one that got away, and now that my life is everything I've always wanted, I need someone to share it with. You wouldn't even have to work in a bar; you could go to school if you want."

I pinch the bridge of my nose, searching for patience somewhere deep inside, and come up empty. "I can't have this conversation right now. You should go back to your friends."

"Promise you'll call me tomorrow, and I'll leave you alone tonight."

"Sure. Fine." I'm lying, but he could never read me well enough to know that.

Hoping this conversation is well and truly over, I turn toward the door marked PRIVATE: EMPLOYEES ONLY, but Law lays a hand on my shoulder and spins me back around before his lips slam down on mine. Completely stunned by the fact that he's pulling some kind of alpha move, it takes me a few seconds before I push him away.

"Whoa. Hey. What the hell?"

I can taste the alcohol he's been drinking, which explains his sudden display of masculinity.

"Needed to give you something to think about."

"Got it. Thinking. Go back to your friends, Law."

With a self-satisfied smile, he gives me a jerk of his chin before he trudges up the stairs. I wait until he's halfway up and shoots me a backward glance before I unlock the storage room and slip inside.

I slump against the door and stare up at the ceiling.

Seriously? Tonight, of all nights.

Law's words echo in my head like a slap. *"You wouldn't even have to work in a bar; you could go to school if you want."* Me working as a bartender is still not up to his standards, obviously. And if I were considering going back to him for even a second, that would ensure a big fat *nope* of a response from me.

This is who I am. If that's not good enough for anyone, they can go fuck themselves.

With a grunt of frustration, I lift the keg Hope asked for off the floor and maneuver the door open with my elbow, then hip check it shut before setting the keg on the floor and making sure the door locks behind me.

The stairs look even steeper now that I have a keg to lug up them, but tonight, I'm all about proving I can do whatever I put my mind to, even if it's as simple as moving something from point A to point B.

I have worth. I have something to offer, I remind myself, even though I feel like a bottom-feeder right now.

As I get to the top of the stairs, Law is waiting near the end of the bar with his friends. When he sees me, he charges toward me.

"Hey, let me help with that, babe." He reaches out to snatch the keg from my arms.

The sudden loss of the weight throws me off-balance and I stumble backward . . . right down the stairs.

I'm too stunned to tuck and roll. No, I just flop and tumble, my arms and legs flailing until I crash to a stop at the bottom, jamming my legs against the floor.

Oh. My. God.

I just fell down a flight of stairs. I could have died.

But I didn't.

I'm okay.

Maybe I don't have the world's worst luck.

"Oh God. Ripley! Are you okay?"

It's Law, already on his way down the stairs as I stumble to my feet, my head swimming.

"I'm fine. It's okay."

I take one dizzy step forward, but when my ankle rolls and pain shoots up my leg, my stomach drops. I instantly take the weight off my leg as tears spring to my eyes.

No. No. No. This can't happen.

Law rushes toward me, skidding to a stop. "Shit. Are you okay?" He pats me down for injuries, not noticing that I'm holding the railing to avoid putting my weight on both feet.

I grit my teeth. "Fine. Totally fine."

"Are you sure? That was a hell of a fall."

I look up the stairs to see if anyone else noticed, but no one else is rushing to the rescue.

"I'm fine. I gotta get that keg to Brian and get back to work."

He reaches out a hand. "Let me help you up the stairs. Seriously, that looked really bad. You're lucky you didn't hurt yourself."

I bite down on my lip to stop myself from groaning as I take the first step up the stairs. Law is too busy talking about how bad my fall looked to realize that I'm seconds from crying.

Breathing through the pain, I hobble my way up and stop next to the keg at the top, sweat beading on my forehead from the effort.

"You sure you don't need help?"

"Positive. I gotta get back to work."

Without waiting for him to respond, I heft the keg into my arms again, screaming inwardly as a shaft of pain stabs at my ankle.

I thought I was lucky? Not a chance.

I manage to get the keg behind the bar and swap it out. Brian gives me a nod of approval, which helps restore a bit of my pride but doesn't do a thing to help my ankle. Hope returns and tosses another tank to me, and I catch it in midair.

"Go change. I'll cover you for a few. Rudy is coming in too. It's almost ten, so this place is gonna be hoppin' in a bit."

The bar is already packed, so I can only imagine how crazy it's going to get.

I take the new uniform shirt and slowly make my way to the break room and employee bathrooms, hoping no one notices that I'm hobbling like an old lady.

If it's broken, I'm screwed. To work behind a bar like this one, you have to be on your toes, bouncing from end to end, making sure the customers keep drinking and handing over tips.

Stop it, Ripley. No more looking at the negative. It's not broken. Everything will be fine after you put some ice on it tonight.

As soon as I reach the break room, I drop onto the couch and survey my already bruising skin. I poke gingerly at it and wince at the sharp pain.

It probably isn't broken, but *damn,* does it hurt. It's swelling, and an entire night working on it is the worst thing I can possibly do. But what choice do I have?

None.

This is when I suck it up and do my job because I'm not about to let Hope down on my first night.

I dig four ibuprofen out of the first aid kit and dry swallow them before changing into my new shirt.

Let's hope they kick in quick.

Then I get my ass back to work.

THIRTY-FIVE

Boone

THE FIRST PLACE I GO TO LOOK FOR RIPLEY IS THE Fishbowl, and I'm praying it isn't closed. The flickering neon sign is lit up, which gives me hope.

Pulling my ball cap lower on my head, I duck inside and find it's a little busier than the first time Frisco and I came in, but definitely nothing like last night when we packed the place.

It doesn't take a genius to guess that some of these people are here hoping Frisco and I will come in again and put on another show. *Sorry, guys. Not happening tonight.*

I stride toward the bar but almost miss a step when I see Ripley's cousin behind it instead of Ripley. Brandy's pouring drinks with an annoyed expression on her face.

Maybe pissed off she finally has to work?

I stop at the end of the bar, and she comes toward me.

"What do you want?"

"Need to talk to Ripley."

The edges of Brandy's mouth curl up smugly. "Well,

you came to the wrong place for that."

Her scathing tone triggers alarm bells in my head.

"What do you mean?"

"Ripley don't work here no more. Uncle Frank fired her. He put me in charge, which means I can tell you to get the hell out."

Ripley's dad fired her? Shit.

"Where is she?"

"Don't know. Don't care. It ain't fair that I got stuck with the mess she left, but that's what I got. So unless you're here to apologize for breaking my phone or to give me another grand to make up for it, you can march your ass right out."

"Is she still living upstairs?"

"No. When I said she's gone, I meant *gone.*"

"And you don't have a clue where she went? I find that hard to believe."

Brandy's lips press into a thin, flat line, and I know she's not going to help me. Unless . . .

I pull out my wallet and peel off a hundred, even though the last thing I want to do is give her a dime. I hold it up in the air, and she crosses her arms over her scrawny chest.

Looking down the bar at the regulars I remember from the other night, I decide to try them instead.

After I reintroduce myself to them, I ask, "Do you have any idea where Ripley might have gone?"

The older woman—Pearl, I think her name is—shakes her head. "Nope. First time in years I haven't seen her behind the bar. There were a couple times when she had strep throat or a cold and didn't want us to catch it, but other than that, she was always here."

While interesting, her information isn't helpful.

My gaze shifts to her husband, Earl. "Any idea?"

He sips his beer. "No, sir."

From the corner of the bar, the bird says, "*You're fired.*"

Brandy giggles from behind the bar. "He's been saying that all day. Just like Uncle Frank."

A sick, sinking feeling takes up residence in my gut.

This is my fault.

I've done nothing but bring shit into Ripley's life that she didn't ask for.

After backing up a few steps, I peel off another hundred and slap both bills on the bar.

"Where the hell is she?"

Brandy reaches out to snatch the cash from beneath my hand, but I keep it pressed tight against the wood.

Her expression twists into something ugly. "I don't care where she is, as long as she's gone. But for two hundred, I'll tell ya that she probably ran to her friend Hope for help. She manages the White Horse."

Brandy yanks at the money again, and I wait a beat before I let it go.

"Good luck keeping this place open without her."

She sneers at me as I turn to head for the door. "I don't need her. I just needed her out of the way."

I spin on my heel, staring her down as I stalk back to the bar and lean over it, getting in her space. "What the fuck did you do?"

Brandy shrugs. "Nothing you can prove."

I haul in a breath and force myself to walk away without saying another word. I want to rip that girl a new one, but it's not gonna help me any.

I shove open the door so hard, it slams against the brick outside before swinging closed behind me.

At least I know where I'm going next.

THIRTY-SIX

Ripley

MY ANKLE BURNS ENOUGH TO KEEP TEARS STINGING behind my eyes with every step, but I keep moving anyway, because that's what you do when you have no other option.

As I serve drinks, the only thing keeping my fake smile in place is the amount of tips I'm pulling in. Even though we split them, I'm going to make more tonight off tips alone than I've ever paid myself in a week at the Fishbowl.

Maybe I should have done this a long time ago.

Thankfully, I don't have time to question my misplaced loyalty because a flurry of drink orders is hurled across the bar by customers.

When I slide two plastic cups under the taps, a guy leans forward and yells, "Are you the chick who fucked Boone Thrasher? Because you look just like the picture I saw online. You're hot. I can totally see why he'd nail you."

I'd been getting some intense looks for the last couple

of hours, but I assumed they were in appreciation of my decent rack in this tight tank top.

Please tell me I wasn't wrong.

"Sorry. Don't know what you're talking about."

He holds out his phone, and on the front page of a massive gossip blog is the picture that little punk-ass Vandy kid snapped last night.

The one that Boone was supposed to take care of.

I can only guess that my expression is one of shock and horror, which the guy takes for an affirmative reply.

"Totally thought so. When you get sick of him, there are plenty of us who'll get in line for a shot at you next. He has killer taste."

"Hey, asshole, that's my girlfriend you're talking to!" Law shouts, slurring his words.

I squeeze my eyes shut with an *are you kidding me* sigh, and flip the taps before removing the full plastic cups from beneath. As much as I want to toss them in his face, I go with my canned reply because *I need this job.*

"Here are your beers, sir. Enjoy your night at the White Horse."

I step away from the bar as Law talks shit to the guy, which has to be an alcohol-fueled development, because whenever some guy would make a comment to me before, he never got upset.

Finally, I lose my grip on my temper and smack a palm on the bar, getting the attention of both men. "Listen up." I point at Law. "Ex-girlfriend, and you don't need to defend my honor. I'm all set." I swing my finger to point at the other guy. "I'll serve you drinks until you run out of money or the laws of the state of Tennessee tell me to stop, but other than that, you aren't getting shit from me. Both of you, step out of the way so I can serve more customers."

The slow clap coming from just behind Law catches my attention, right before the source starts speaking.

"Good to know I'm not the only one who gets the sharp side of your tongue, sugar."

The deep voice, rough and husky, has both men I just bitched out spinning around.

"Whoa. Holy shit. You're Boone Thrasher."

Boone's blue eyes pierce the punk. "And you're a piece of shit. Don't talk to my girl again if you want to walk out of here."

His girl? Uh, say what now?

Boone's gaze swings to Law, dealing with them one at a time like I just did. "Don't know who you think you are, but it doesn't matter to me."

Finally, Boone meets my eyes. Lowering his voice, he says, "What are you doing here?"

"Working! Can we please talk about whatever's on your mind later, superstar, because I'm a little busy."

I snag two more plastic cups and shove them under the taps. For a minute, I think Boone is going to tell me no, we're going to talk right now, but he doesn't.

"Fine. I know how I can pass a few hours."

He glances toward the stage where the house band is taking a break after their first set.

Hope comes toward me, taking in Boone and Law. "Oh hell, isn't this a fun little reunion?"

"You Hope?" Boone asks, and she nods. "Mind if I borrow your stage for a while?"

I glance at her as her face lights up.

"Hell no, I don't mind. We broke our record the night you and Frisco crashed last week. Bring it on, man."

Boone nods. "Thanks. I gotta wait until Rip here finishes her shift, so I might as well make it fun."

Hope steals one of the beers I'm pouring and hands it across the bar to Boone. "On the house. Go tear it up. I'll get security for you and have them call in a bigger crew."

Boone's gaze shifts back to me. "I like your friend."

Without another word, Boone turns and makes his way through the crowd until he hits the stage. He jumps up on it, beer in one hand as he grabs the microphone with the other. He takes a swig and waits for the house music to stop before he speaks into it.

"How y'all doin' tonight?"

The crowd on the floor turns in unison to stare at Boone before erupting into screams and cheers.

"I had so much fun here the other night, I thought I'd come back and do it again."

Someone starts the chant, and suddenly the bar is filled with people yelling, "Boone! Boone! Boone!"

Hope turns to me, and over the din, she says, "He is *hot* for you. Ride that train for all it's worth, baby girl."

An hour later, my ankle is swollen to the size of a grapefruit, and I can't pretend it doesn't hurt like hell. I'm limping toward my next customer when Brian drops a hand on my shoulder.

"What the fuck happened to you?"

"Rolled my ankle on the stairs."

His eyes widen. "When you got the keg? And you've

been walking on it this whole time without saying a damn thing?"

"It's my first night. I wasn't about to complain when I need this job."

Brian shakes his head like I just told him I slammed my hand in a door on purpose. "You're an idiot. What good will you be tomorrow if you don't take care of it?"

"I don't have a shift until Wednesday. Hope is working me into the schedule, so I need the money from tonight to . . . well, I need it."

"I get it. But you need to get off that ankle. I'll get Hope."

He strides away, says something to Hope, and my friend hustles toward me.

"You little asshole, why didn't you tell me?"

"Really? You know why."

"Fine, but you're done. I'll grab my keys and you can take my truck home. I'll get a ride with someone else. I'll be back in two minutes." She rushes away toward the employee break room and her locker, and I keep serving drinks.

When Hope returns, she hands me her keys. "Are you gonna be okay driving and walking on that?"

It's my left ankle, so as long as I don't have to drive a manual transmission *like my own freaking car*, I'll be fine.

"I'm good."

"We'll split all of tonight's tips at close, and I'll bring yours home."

"Give me a smaller share. I'm leaving early."

"Shut up."

"Love you."

"Love you more. Go get your shit and get out of here."

I duck into the break room and when I come out, I notice one major difference—Boone's voice is no longer carrying through the bar. Instead, another top country hit is coming through the speakers.

Hope is already hard at work, so I limp toward the back door.

More accurately, I *start* to limp toward the back door.

"What the fuck?" Boone's voice booms from behind me. "Are you okay? What happened?"

Glancing back toward the bar, I see him with a bottle of water in one hand, and security on either side of him.

The last thing I need is another public scene at my brand-new job.

"Nothing. I'm heading out." I take another step, attempting not to limp, but a hiss of pain escapes my lips.

Boone is on me faster than I can silence it.

"What happened, sugar? And don't lie to me."

I bite my lip, debating for a hot second whether to tell him the truth.

"Ripley . . ."

When he says my name with an edge to it, I decide I'll get out of here quicker if I just tell him.

"I fell down the stairs and rolled my ankle right before you got here. It's swelling up, so I'm going back to Hope's to put some ice on it."

Boone's expression morphs from one of concern to anger in the flash of a second. "You fell down the fucking stairs and you've been working for over a goddamned hour on a sprained ankle? Behind a bar?"

My jaw clenched, I reply. "I'm trying to leave now, so if you'll—"

"You need to go to a hospital and make sure it ain't broken. Fell down the stairs. Jesus Christ, woman."

It's on the tip of my tongue to tell him *not freaking happening, because I don't have health insurance*, but instead I wave him off.

"I'll be fine at Hope's. I just need to put some ice on it."

Boone's eyes meet mine, his expression somber yet frustrated. "Let me help you."

If there's one trait I got from Pop, it's my stubbornness. "I'm fine. I'm going now." I step around Boone but he spins, bends down, and drops his shoulder to my stomach and lifts me up.

"What—"

"The only place you're going is with me."

One of the security guys chuckles as Boone strides out of the bar with me over his shoulder, ignoring my protests to put me down.

"Hey, asshole. She said put her down."

I recognize Law's voice, but Boone doesn't slow.

Security keeps everyone back, and we clear the door. From my position over his shoulder, I can't see a thing, but once we're outside, I can hear yelling.

My name. His name. Questions.

Shit. It's the press. They found him, and now pictures of me dangling over his shoulder like some barbarian conqueror's prize will be all over the internet. Freaking fabulous.

I renew my struggles. "Put me down! They're going to get pic—"

Boone lowers me to the ground, cutting off my demand as he wraps an arm around me. "Hold on to me for balance. Try not to put any weight on that ankle."

How can he sound so normal?

Trying not to look toward the flashing cameras, I finally realize we're standing next to Boone's car, which is parked in a prime location behind the bar. Someone set up portable barricades like you would see outside a concert venue for crowd control, and three uniformed security guards stand with their arms crossed. The flashing cameras and shouting voices are beyond the wall of metal and muscle.

"They're getting pictures of us together. Of you carrying me. Don't you care? And did they really put a fence around your car? This is all crazy." My hair, which was in a messy bun on top of my head, is now tangled around my shoulders.

Boone unlocks the car before shifting his attention back to me. He searches my face, but I don't have a clue what he's looking for. Finally, he speaks.

"You're in my life, Ripley. It doesn't matter how it happened, but it happened. Do I wish the press didn't come with me? Sure, but it's something I deal with. Am I going to let them stop me from doing what I want? Not a chance. It might be a little crazy, but maybe I am too—about you."

Boone spears his fingers through my hair and cups the back of my head. His blue eyes flash before he lowers his mouth to mine.

My brain is telling my body to pull away. To stop him before the reporters get more ammunition to use against me. But my body flips my brain the bird and curls into Boone and his kiss.

When he finally pulls back, he studies my face again. "I've been wanting to do that all night. Let's get you in the car so we can get out of here."

Boone maneuvers me into the front seat and shuts the door. The questions from the press are muted now that I'm inside the car, and I can almost forget they're out there. *Almost.*

When Boone finally climbs inside and fires up the engine, the security guards move the metal barriers to make room for the car to fit through. They do a good enough job keeping the press corralled so we can get by. Boone snags Hope's keys from my hand and rolls down the window to toss them to a bald security guy.

"Take these to the head bartender inside. Thanks, man."

Once we're on the road, Boone revs the engine and hauls ass down the street.

That's when it occurs to me that I have no clue where we're going.

THIRTY-SEVEN

Boone

THE LYRICS TO MY NEW SINGLE STREAM THROUGH MY head with Ripley sitting in the front seat.

I'm gonna take a ride with you
in my 442.
Rolling down the same old roads
like we always do.
Other things may change,
my love remains the same.
With you by my side
in my new old ride,
in my 442.

I'd written that song thinking that it would be Amber rolling down the back roads with me, but she's never even been inside this car. It was delivered the night before I planned to propose. The night she married someone else.

The burn might still be fresh, but tonight it's not

causing me any pain at all.

"Where are we going?" Ripley asks.

I shake off the thoughts of Amber, not wanting tonight polluted with her.

"First, to the ER so you can get that ankle looked at."

Ripley's expression turns panicked. "No, we're not. I can't afford it. Besides, I don't need a doctor to tell me I sprained my ankle and I need to stay off it for a day, put some ice on it, and keep it elevated."

Despite her protests, I turn toward the hospital.

"You're stubborn enough to lose an arm and tell me you only need a Band-Aid, so I don't care what you think you need. I'm telling you you're gettin' it x-rayed. We don't know how bad it really is yet."

Ripley shoots me a glare. "If I lost an arm, I'd be begging to go to a hospital. I'm not an idiot." Her tone is snappish, but I figure that's better than the panic I saw on her face before.

"I didn't say you were. I said you were stubborn. But guess what? So am I."

She stares straight ahead, her voice almost inaudible over the growl of my big-block engine. "Look, I'm not just being contrary. I can't go the ER. I don't have insurance. I don't have enough cash. I just . . . I can't. Not right now. I'll be fine. Just take me back to Hope's, and I can wait for her in my car."

Is she fucking serious? She can't mean that. I glance over at Ripley, her spine ramrod straight and shoulders back, her chin lifted.

I was wrong. It's not stubbornness, it's pride. My girl has it in spades.

"I'm covering the bill. We both know you're working at the White Horse instead of the Fishbowl because of me." I reach over and lay a hand on her thigh. "I'm sorry, Ripley. It wasn't my intent to get you fired and kicked out of your apartment. I—"

She shifts toward me in the passenger seat. "I quit. He didn't fire me until after I said I quit. So I'm going to stick to my story. And as for getting kicked out of the apartment, I'll figure it out. It's . . . it's been a long time coming, if you want to know the truth. It wasn't your fault. Friday night might have been the last shove over the edge, but it's certainly not the only reason. Don't go feeling guilty because I'm homeless and jobless. I don't need your pity."

I squeeze her leg. "The last thing I feel toward you is pity. But I do feel responsible, and I'm not shirking that responsibility. You're just gonna have to deal with that."

I finally move my hand and make a right at the glowing EMERGENCY ROOM sign. Ripley looks at me, her face screwed up in irritation.

"I'm not going inside."

"Then I'll be carrying you again."

"What part of *no* don't you understand?"

"Any of it when it means you don't take care of yourself. So, stop arguing with me and deal with it."

Ripley keeps up with the protests as I park the car, when I open her door and lift her into my arms, and all the way through the sliding glass doors.

The woman at the triage desk looks up for a beat before going back to her paperwork. But in *three . . . two . . . one . . .* she jerks her gaze up again for a double-take and her eyes widen.

"Can you get us into a private room?"

Her mouth opens, but no words come out. She finds her voice a moment later. "Yes. Of course, Mr. Thrasher. Please come with me." She glances to another woman working at the desk. "I'll be right back."

Within moments, we're in an exam room, and I lower Ripley onto the hospital bed.

"Let me get Dr. Marks for you. I'll be right back." She closes the door behind her.

"This is seriously what it's like to be you? I mean, you just walk in and people rush to do whatever you need? Wow. I took the wrong career path, because it might be worth it, if only to skip the lines everywhere you go."

Heat flashes at the base of my neck because she's right. This *is* what it's like to be me. At least, now it is.

"It wasn't always like this. Trust me. And I don't feel bad about using it to my advantage when I need to, like right now."

Ripley looks like she's going to say something else, but there's a knock on the door before it opens a crack. A woman in a white coat with a stethoscope around her neck steps inside.

She reaches out a hand. "Mr. Thrasher, I'm Dr. Marks. What can we do for you today?"

Ripley rolls her eyes at the deferential tone, and it occurs to me that I've gotten used to being treated like this. It's not a surprise anymore. I'm not sure how I feel about the fact that I've been taking this kind of service for granted. My mama would kick my ass if she knew.

"Ms. Fischer sprained her ankle, or maybe broke it, we're not sure. She needs an X-ray. Can you take a look?"

Dr. Marks smiles at both of us. "Of course, Mr. Thrasher. We'll take great care of Ms. Fischer."

The deferential treatment continues for the entire sixty minutes we're in the ER. We're in and out of radiology in moments, and the X-ray reveals her ankle is sprained. Ripley is fitted with an Aircast and given a prescription for some painkillers. The hospital staff apologizes profusely for being out of crutches in Ripley's size, for which I'm partially grateful because I know she'd overdo if she could get around.

Before we leave, I fill out a form to have the bill sent to my financial manager to be handled. Through all of this, Ripley stays quiet, only giving the information requested of her. At least until they bring the wheelchair to take her out.

"I'll pass, thank you."

The man who wheeled it into the room frowns. "Ma'am, I'm afraid we'll have to insist."

"It's either this or I'll carry you again," I tell her. I figure Ripley will have her ass in that chair so fast, the orderly's head will spin. Not so.

Ripley looks up at me. "No wheelchair."

I don't hesitate to lift her into my arms. Call it primal, but I like carrying her around.

When the orderly protests, Dr. Marks gives him a silencing look before turning back to me. "If you'd like, we can have someone bring your car around and you can go out the back entrance."

"I appreciate it, but that's not necessary. We're all set."

Just when I think that there's no chance the media could have gotten wind of us being here already, I'm proven wrong. As soon as we step out of the glass doors, a camera flashes.

Ripley stiffens in my arms, burying her face against my chest.

"It's okay. It's just one guy. He'll get a few photos and probably try to tail us."

"This is ridiculous."

"I'm not usually such a big draw. I swear it's not always like this."

I glance down at her, and I think Ripley gets what I'm saying. The mess with Amber and then the press latching onto Ripley and me has made me way more entertaining copy that I've been in the last year. The happy-couple stories get old. What the media wants is drama.

He follows us at a distance all the way to the car, watching as I get Ripley inside.

After I close the door, I walk over to him. The guy looks a little scared, like I might decide to kick his ass. Valid concern.

"You get everything you need, man?"

His eyes bug out, probably with shock because I'm not yelling. "Uh, yeah. I think so."

I nod. "Good deal. Since you're the only guy I see here, you got your exclusive for the night. We're going home, and I guarantee there won't be shit for you to see because we'll be behind gates and trees. Save yourself some time and don't bother following us. There's no point."

"You're going back to your place. With the girl? You together? What's the deal with that?" He launches into a bunch of questions that I have no intention of answering.

"I told you all I'm gonna tell you, so I'd really appreciate it if you'd move on, man."

He yanks a card from his pocket and holds it out. "If you ever want to—"

I look down at it, and part of me wants to rip him a new one for overstepping, but I'm too tired tonight. I take it from him and shove it in my pocket.

"Have a good one."

"You too, Mr. Thrasher. I hope Ms. Fischer is okay."

"She'll be fine."

THIRTY-EIGHT

Ripley

I'VE SPENT THE LAST DECADE AS A NIGHT OWL, SO being awake at three thirty in the morning isn't unusual. But now I'm exhausted—physically, mentally, and emotionally.

When Boone heads away from town, I don't have the fortitude to argue with him about where I'm sleeping, because I have a feeling I would probably lose.

Even with the outcome a foregone conclusion, any other night I would put up a fight. Tonight, I'm *done.*

"If they never find my body, you know they'll come after you," I tell him as he merges onto the highway. "That paparazzi guy will make sure of it."

Boone's eyes shift away from the road to me, shafts of light sliding across his face as the 442 accelerates. "You trying to say you think I'm a serial killer?"

I shake my head before dropping it back against the seat. "No. I'm just tired. It's been a long day."

"You wanna tell me what went down with your dad?"

I squeeze my eyes shut, not wanting to replay that memory anytime soon. "Nope."

"You wanna tell me about the douchebag in the bar?"

I open my eyes a tad and check out Boone's expression. "Law? Not really."

"*Law*?"

I snort-chuckle at the way Boone says his name. "Yeah, short for Lawrence. He's wanted to be a lawyer since he was a kid, so instead of going by his full name, he shortened it."

"I was right. Total douchebag. And you dated him?"

Apparently, Boone didn't catch my *not really*. I could choose not to answer, but he would badger me anyway.

"Yes."

"For how long?"

"A little over a year."

"And?" Boone changes lanes before taking the next exit.

"And what? We dated. Then we were done."

His pointed look tells me that there's no way in hell he believes it was that simple. "There's more to the story than that."

Wanting to move on to a new subject, I give him the quick-and-dirty rundown. "He was in law school and I worked at the Fishbowl. Not only did our schedules not mesh, he wanted me to choose between him and the bar. So I did."

Boone slows at a stoplight ahead. "Why didn't you choose the bar this time?"

I look up at the red headliner because his question is a valid one. Every time I've been forced to choose between anything or anyone and the bar, I've chosen the Fishbowl.

"I don't know." My tone is quiet and thoughtful.

We don't speak for the rest of the drive. When we pull up in front of an eight-foot-tall black metal gate, Boone slows and it swings open.

"Sensor in the car," he explains.

I nod like that makes perfect sense, but automatic gates have never been part of my life. I can see why he'd need one given what he puts up with, though. The house doesn't come into view for a good two minutes as we cruise up the long driveway through a field and then woods. Tucked away in the middle of what must be a massive piece of property is a sprawling rock-and-wood structure that looks like it would merit an episode of CMT's *Cribs*.

"Damn. You couldn't build something a *little* bigger?"

Boone laughs. "You sound like my brother. He gives me shit every time he's here. Like why didn't I build an indoor pool? Or a tennis court? It's not like a bowling lane is enough entertainment."

"You have a bowling lane?"

I blink as a massive garage door opens and he drives the 442 inside to park next to a huge black truck that looks like it cost more than the building the Fishbowl is located in.

"I'll show you tomorrow. Sit tight; I'm coming around to get you."

But I don't. I open the car door and climb out, hopping on one foot and using the truck for balance. I'd feel bad about leaving fingerprints on it, but the mud on the tires tells me Boone's not going to care.

At least, not about the truck.

"I told you to wait, dammit." Before I protest, I'm

cradled in Boone's arms again and he carries me into the house.

It's dark, but when he flips on the lights, my mouth slackens. It's *gorgeous.*

"Holy shit."

"Yeah, I know. If someone had left all the designing up to me, I probably would've had antlers everywhere, but my decorator put the smackdown on that."

He brings me through a huge mud room, an insanely gorgeous kitchen that I barely have time to appreciate, and down a long hallway with a high ceiling. At the end of the hall, he walks into a massive bedroom with what has to be a California king in the center with a frame made of logs and leather.

It's so completely Boone.

"Wow. This is . . . nice." Inwardly I'm cringing, thinking about the fact that he was in my shitty little apartment.

But at least you had your apartment then. Now your stuff is in boxes and a duffel bag next to a futon in your best friend's living room.

The world of difference between our situations couldn't be more obvious, and yet Boone isn't flashy about his money. Law had waited a whole thirty seconds before he told me his salary to try to impress me. I've never heard Boone talk about money . . . ever.

Maybe that's because he has so much, it's not something he even thinks about.

Boone lowers me onto the bed. "You're staying in here."

"But this is your room." My tone takes on a hint of panic.

"Good eye."

"I can't stay in here. With you."

Boone crosses both arms over his chest. "Why the hell not?"

"Because I can't. That's not—It just—I can't."

Boone tugs off his ball cap and drops it on top of a nightstand before running a hand through his shaggy brown hair. "It's too late to argue about this. Let's wash up, get some sleep, and figure it out in the morning."

I'm not trying to be ungrateful—really, I'm not—but I can't share a bed with Boone. I know we slept together, but this is intimacy on a whole different level.

"But—"

"You've got a sprained ankle and you're wearing a damn Aircast. It's not like I'm gonna try to fuck you tonight, Rip. We both need sleep."

My nipples, traitorous little bitches that they are, perk up when he says *try to fuck you*. Boone doesn't miss it.

"No matter how bad I want to."

The heat blazing in his blue eyes sears me. For long moments, I meet his stare, and with each passing second, that heat spreads through my body.

What is it about this man that sets me off like no one ever has before? It's not fair that I have no control over my physical reactions when it comes to Boone.

I swallow, wishing he'd say something.

"You're killing me, sugar. You keep looking at me like that, and I won't be able to keep my word." His tone is husky, dripping with promise, and I'm seconds away from giving in.

Surprisingly, Boone breaks our stare first, turning and jamming his hands in his pockets. When he turns back around a few moments later, the heat is banked.

"I'll carry you into the bathroom and you can do your thing. Holler if you need any help. There's probably an extra toothbrush in the bottom drawer. Housekeeper stashes them in every bathroom."

Without any more discussion, he picks me up off the bed and takes me to a bathroom bigger than my apartment. Well, my old apartment. After Boone carefully lowers my feet to the floor, he shuts the door behind me, and I hobble to the toilet and sit down on the lid.

What am I doing here?

Taking a deep breath, I pull up my metaphorical big-girl panties and do what I need to do. With my face washed and teeth brushed, I open the door to find Boone tossing a T-shirt and sweats on the bed. Both massive.

"You can change while I'm in there." He picks me up and moves me back to the bed before tossing the clothes closer to me. "This is the best I could do on short notice. I'll be back in a few." The words are stilted, missing the easiness I'm used to from him.

Boone disappears into the bathroom and I hastily change. The T-shirt is like a dress on me, the same size as the one he put on me when I was drunk that night outside the White Horse, so I forgo the sweatpants. It might be a bad idea, but they're way too big.

I eye the bed. *This is a terrible idea.* But I climb under the covers anyway, and pull them up to my chin.

My brilliant plan includes pretending to be asleep by the time he gets out of the bathroom, but I don't have to fake it. Exhaustion pulls me under in record time.

THIRTY-NINE

Boone

A STREAK OF POSSESSIVENESS FLASHES THROUGH ME when I see Ripley sound asleep in the middle of my bed.

I never felt like that with Amber, probably because she didn't like this room and insisted on staying in one of the guest suites on the rare occasion she spent the night here.

The more insights I have like this about Amber, the more I understand that I dodged a bullet. My pride may have taken a beating, but I was lucky it happened the way it did. I was so caught up with the idea of having someone who was only mine, and starting a family and building a life together, that I was blind to the fact that the person I picked wasn't the right one.

As always, Ma knew better.

When I slide under the covers and turn on my side, Ripley's sleeping form snuggles into my body so that my chest presses against her back. I wrap my arm around her, and the tension in my body releases.

Before I can think about why that is, I'm out too.

The sun beats down on me, and I toss the covers off, trying to escape the heat. *The heat.*

I jerk awake, expecting to see a dark-haired wildcat in bed beside me, but she's gone.

Did I dream all that?

I catch sight of the sweatpants I'd offered her last night still folded up on the foot of the bed.

No. Definitely not a dream.

Which means that my wildcat is somewhere limping around my house when she's supposed to be staying off her ankle so it can heal.

I bolt out of bed and head for the door. Normally I'd stop to grab some clothes because I usually sleep buck-ass naked, but last night, out of courtesy for Ripley, I put on some gym shorts. I follow my nose into the kitchen, but I can't place the scent.

Ripley lifts a basket out of the fryer and drops fresh golden lumps onto a paper-towel-covered plate.

Holy shit. Is she making donuts?

My morning wood turns into a full hard-on, and not only because she's wearing just my shirt, which skims the top of her thighs when she reaches up into the cupboard.

Sweet Lord, I don't know what I did to deserve this, but I promise I'm gonna do it again real soon.

Ripley turns and startles when she sees me, dropping a bag of powdered sugar on the counter. A puff of white escapes from the bag as she slaps a hand over her chest.

"Jesus, you scared the shit out of me. A man your size

shouldn't be able to move that quietly."

"Did you seriously make donuts? From scratch?"

"Yeah."

I take a step closer. "I should have brought you home a long time ago."

I stop less than a foot in front of her, and *fuck*, she smells amazing. If women wore donut-scented perfume, I guarantee they'd have to beat men off.

"I need to drop these last three in so I can finish up and make the icing."

Lowering my head to bring my lips an inch away from her temple, I tell her, "As sexy as you look right now, wearing nothing but my T-shirt and making one of my favorite foods, you need to get out of the kitchen and off that ankle."

Her breath ghosts across my skin, which doesn't help my hard-on.

"I've been sitting while they fry." She jerks her head toward the bar stool behind her.

I pick her up and put her on the stool. "I'll finish them."

She lifts her head, and I can't resist leaning forward to close my teeth over her perfect bottom lip and tug. Ripley freezes. I release her, but my tongue darts out to taste where I nipped.

"You're so fucking sexy. You taste like you've already gotten into the donuts," I tell her, not wanting to back away yet. "I want you, Ripley. Really fucking bad. If you'd still been in my bed when I woke up, you'd have my cock buried inside you right now, and I'd be making you scream."

Her breathing quickens, and I lift my hand to trail it along the skin of her leg, inching the shirt up as I go higher.

"You like that?"

Her nod barely registers as a movement.

"If I reach between these gorgeous legs, am I gonna find a wet pussy?"

She doesn't answer, instead swallows audibly.

"No answer? I guess I'm gonna have to find out for myself."

I curve my hand around the top of her luscious *naked* ass, squeezing a handful and releasing a groan. "Do you have any idea how sexy it is that you're never wearing any panties? *Jesus.*"

"I . . ."

Whatever she's going to say trails off when I slide a hand between her thighs and cup her hot, wet center.

"Sweet fucking Christ, woman." I push the tips of two fingers inside, and Ripley arches toward me.

"Screw the donuts. This can't wait."

FORTY

Ripley

OH. MY. GOD.

Boone's fingering me in his kitchen—and it's amazing.

My hips jerk, seeking more contact, deeper, harder, faster. I don't care what he does, but I need him to do more of it.

"Please," I whisper, even though I hate to beg.

"You could ask me for anything right now, and I'd give it to you." His voice is deep and gravelly, and my nipples peak against the T-shirt.

"I need . . . more."

Boone's blue eyes search my face. "Sugar, I'm gonna give you everything."

He pulls his fingers away and palms my ass with both hands, lifting me off the bar stool. He carries me to the huge farmhouse-style table six feet from the kitchen, and sets me on the cool wood.

"This is the kind of breakfast I could get used to." He

lowers his head, closes his mouth around the hard bud through the cotton, and sucks.

Electricity pulses and shoots through my body, lighting up my senses, my injured ankle all but forgotten.

With his other hand, Boone shoves the T-shirt up and slides a finger inside me.

One long, thick finger.

I arch, leaning back on my elbows as Boone plays my body with as much skill as his guitar onstage. His teeth nip, tugging at my nipple the same way he did my lip, and a moan escapes my throat.

He releases it before whipping the shirt up and over my head. "So much better."

Back to his ministrations, he sucks at the other peak, hardening them both into tight buds.

It's not going to happen. Not yet. That's impossible.

And yet the rush of an impending orgasm builds in my veins, threatening to take me under.

"More." It comes out sounding like a plea and a demand, and is met by a growl from Boone's lips as his finger plunges inside harder and faster, his thumb finding my clit.

"Yes. Yes. *Yes.*" My entire body goes taut, and my vision turns fuzzy as my eyes roll back in my head. The release washes over me, and my entire body turns languid.

If this is what I get for making donuts in the morning, I'm one hundred percent down with being Betty freaking Crocker.

"Your tight little cunt doesn't want to let my finger go."

Normally the C-word would put my back up, but on Boone's lips right now, it's hotter than I could have imagined.

My eyes fix on the outline of his massive erection

against his gym shorts, and I want it.

Boone follows the direction of my gaze, and his lips tug into a sinful smile. He pulls his finger free of my pussy and lifts it to his mouth, sucking my juices clean. "You taste so damned good."

It's primitive, the feeling that's gripping every cell in my body.

"Hurry."

Boone shoves down his shorts and wraps a hand around his thick cock and squeezes. "Can you take it all? Everything I've got to give? As hard as I want?"

My hips lift, anxious to get closer. "Yes."

He steps between my legs, levering them apart with his hips.

"You sure? Because the way you got my blood roaring right now, you're gonna be feeling me tomorrow." His lip quirks up on one side. "I like the thought of that. You, feeling me with every step you take. Remembering what it was like to take my cock hard and fast."

As he speaks the words, he presses closer, rubbing the head through my slick heat.

"Yeah, I like that a hell of a lot. You're gonna go wild for me, aren't you, sugar?"

"I'll give you whatever you want if you'll just—"

At my declaration, his eyes blaze.

"You should be careful offering a man like me whatever I want. I'm not afraid to take it."

With the head of his cock nudging against my opening, Boone grips my hips with both hands.

"So tell me, Ripley, you really mean that? Whatever I want?"

"Yes!" I yell, desperate to have him inside me, and probably willing to agree to anything right now.

"Heaven help you, because I'm not letting you go back on that." With a jerk, Boone yanks my hips toward him and slams forward at the same time, driving his cock deep, almost to the point of discomfort. Since I'm already lit up from my last orgasm, the line between pain and pleasure blurs.

Boone's expression takes on an intensity I've never seen before as he unleashes everything he's been holding back.

He uses his grip on my hips to pull me back and forth until my body is fucking his cock as much as his cock is fucking me. Each pounding thrust takes my breath away, but I've never experienced anything more erotic in my life. My eyelids drift closed, but Boone releases one hip and slaps my thigh, demanding my attention.

"Eyes on me. I want you to know who's fucking you. Whose name you're gonna scream when you come."

And then he becomes relentless, and I'm helpless to do anything but hang on tight and enjoy the ride. His gaze never leaves mine, almost daring me not to come. I hold back for as long as I can, but it's a losing battle.

"Boone!" His name leaves my lips on a hoarse scream as a blinding orgasm rips through my body. I break our stare as my head rocks from side to side, unable to keep still as the pleasure owns every inch of me.

Boone doesn't slow his pace. Sensation overwhelms me as he powers inside me over and over, seeking his own release. When his roar echoes through the room, his cock pulses and I'm filled with heat.

For long moments, the only sound in the room is our heaving breaths. As my brain flips on again, the first thought that rushes through my mind hits harder than a heavyweight.

Oh. Shit.

We didn't use a condom.

FORTY-ONE

Boone

BEFORE THIS MORNING, I'VE NEVER COME SO HARD in my life. It was a near religious experience. Sweat drips from my forehead, and my fingers are still wrapped around Ripley's hips.

I let go immediately when I realize how tight a hold I have on her.

"Crap, did I hurt you?"

A rusty laugh falls from her lips. "Are you joking?"

I shake my head as I inspect the red marks I've left on her skin. "I didn't realize—"

She pushes up on her elbows. "It's fine. But we have a bigger problem."

My gaze cuts to hers. "What?"

She glances down to where I'm still buried balls deep. "No condom."

"Shit."

"Yeah." She shakes her head. "I didn't even think."

"I didn't either. Hell. I'm sorry, sugar. That's all on me."

Her eyebrows dive into a deep vee. "You don't . . . have anything. Do you?"

It takes me a second to realize what she's asking. "No. Fuck no. I'm clean. I always use a condom."

I can tell she wants to ask a question by the way her mouth keeps opening and closing, and given her hesitation, I can guess what it is.

"Even with my ex. She didn't want to take a chance that she'd get pregnant, so we're good. I haven't been with anyone else in two years."

Now her eyebrows wing up in surprise.

"Really?" Her question comes out on a tone of disbelief.

"Yeah. I don't screw around. That's not my style."

"But—I mean, I thought . . ."

This time I raise an eyebrow. "What? That just because I get more pussy thrown my way than a major-league catcher gets balls, I must've cheated on my girlfriend?"

Ripley bites down on her lip but doesn't answer. Her lack of response is enough, though.

"Not a chance. I might be an asshole, but I'm not a cheating asshole."

I pull out, pissed that we're having this conversation while I'm still inside her, ready to get hard again and go for round two. Turning around to head to the kitchen, I snag a paper towel and bring it back to Ripley. It's been so damn long since I've had sex without a condom, I forgot how much of a mess it is.

She takes the paper towel from me, but grabs the T-shirt and pulls it back on first. Her shields go up fast, but it's good to know that I have at least one way I can get her to lower them.

I return to the kitchen, wanting to give her some privacy. And maybe also because the donuts are there. I'm already on my second when she speaks again.

"Crap. The fryer has been on this whole time." She climbs off the table, probably intent on rushing forward, but I stop her with my shoulder against her belly as I lift her up.

Her screech, not nearly as sexy as the sound of her screaming my name, almost blows out my eardrum.

"You're not walking on that ankle." I carry her around to the bar stools pulled up on the other side of the island and settle her on one. "Sit your ass down and put your foot up. I'll finish the donuts. It can't be that hard."

With a frustrated huff, Ripley follows my instructions, which surprises me.

"Easy? Really? Have you ever made donuts before?" Her gray eyes, no longer cloudy with that haze of lust, shoot me a look stamped with challenge.

"You can talk me through it so I don't screw them up."

"And the icing?"

I look at the bag of powdered sugar. "They can be powdered donuts. I'm not Martha frickin' Stewart."

At Ripley's giggle, a smile breaks over my face, but it also reminds me that I didn't ask a question I need an answer to. No point in waiting for later to satisfy my curiosity.

"You on the pill? Or do we need to start wondering if there's gonna be a little Boone running around for my ma to spoil?"

This time, her eyebrows almost hit her hairline.

Surprised I'd want her to have the kid if she got pregnant? Either way, I decide to wait for her response before I attempt donut-making.

"We're good. I'm on the shot." She slaps her hip. "Part of the reason my ass is so damn big."

I narrow my eyes on her. "You better leave your ass alone because I'm a pretty big fucking fan of it. In fact, I got some plans for it."

Her cheeks turn red. "What kind of plans?"

I give her a wink. "I'll let you wonder. Don't want to give it all away."

"I've never . . . done the butt stuff before."

First donuts, then mind-blowing sex on my kitchen table, and now we're diving into anal territory. One hell of a perfect morning, in my book.

A smile tugs on my lips even as I try to hold it back. "What do you mean, *done the butt stuff*?"

Ripley drops her gaze to my granite countertop, tracing a vein. Her response is a mumble. "You know . . . my back door has never been . . . open for business."

Laughter starts deep in my gut and rolls through my body. Ripley grabs a pen off the counter and throws it at my head, but I bat it away.

"Don't laugh at me. It's not like I'm the only one in the world who has never—"

"Had your back door open for business?"

It's not her inexperience that's the reason for my laughter, it's the way she describes it, which only goes to highlight just how genuine that inexperience is.

I lean forward and place both forearms on the counter. "Don't worry, sugar. We'll start with a soft opening."

FORTY-TWO

Ripley

BOONE'S WORDS REPEAT ON A LOOP IN THE BACK OF my mind as I sit in the passenger seat of his giant crew-cab pickup heading downtown to get Esteban.

"Don't worry, sugar. We'll start with a soft opening."

Oh. My. God.

I shift in my seat, trying to pretend the idea isn't physically affecting me.

Boone glances over, a smirk on his face, and I can tell I'm doing a terrible job. He doesn't have to say a word for me to know that we're thinking about the same thing. When he stops at the red light on the exit ramp, he leans over and snakes a hand behind my neck to draw me closer before taking my lips in a hard kiss.

He pulls back when horns honk behind us because the light has turned green.

"They're lucky we've got something to do. I could get lost in your lips for hours. Puttin' that on my priority list real soon."

And that sends a rush of heat that takes up residence between my legs.

Gah. What is it about this guy?

It's not like he says all the right things, because he absolutely *does not.* But somehow, the things he does say affect me in a way that no one else has before.

He's crass. Bold. Straightforward.

None of those things should be new to me because crass, bold, and straightforward are what you get when you grow up working in a bar. But there's something else. Maybe it's the no-bullshit factor. Boone shoots straight with me, and despite *what* he is, I trust him. That's a big one for me. After my mama betrayed our family with Gil, and Pop constantly lied about drinking until he finally stopped giving a shit, and then I had to deal with my cousin's endless tattling, trust isn't something I find easy to give.

But with Boone, I don't see any ulterior motives. Is that why I'm breaking my rule for him?

With Frisco, I wasn't even tempted. Maybe because I could tell he was never serious, and me saying no to him was always more of a game. Plus, there was never the spark. But with Boone, it's more than a spark—it's an inferno threatening to burn down the entire town. And yet, there's something else.

For the first time in my life, I made a completely selfish decision. This thing, whatever we have, is for *me.* To hell with Pop, Brandy, the bar, and everything else, because I've gone too long without doing something solely for myself.

On top of that, something about Boone has me letting my guard down in a way I never thought possible.

He's turned the stereotype I've held on to for so long on its head, and shown me that he's more than an entitled asshole with a record deal and tour buses. He's a guy who keeps showing me he actually gives a shit about me, and goes out of his way to prove it.

I'm not walking into this blind, though, and there's no way I'm dropping my guard completely, but I think it's time I take a risk on something that feels *right*, regardless of the consequences. Because when Boone tells me he's going to take care of things, I actually believe him, and something about that is incredibly seductive.

Maybe I should go back to not thinking about why I'm going against my hard-and-fast rule. That's easier than trying to justify it to myself.

Boone interrupts my thoughts with a question as we get closer to the Fishbowl.

"You got a plan for how you want this birdnapping to go down?"

I shoot him a sidelong glance. "Birdnapping? Really?"

"Just callin' it what it is. The bird ain't yours, but we're taking it whether they like it or not. What else do you want to call it?"

"Bird rescue." To my own ears, I sound determined and defiant.

"Still can't believe you talked me into this." Boone's tone carries a hint of exasperation.

I shift in my seat again as I remember what I promised him in return.

"You help me get Esteban out of the bar, and I'll let you do whatever kind of opening you want on my back door."

I'm not even sure what to call that. I officially offered

up my anal virginity to a guy for helping me steal a bird.

Desperate times.

My brain smacks me down. *Quit lying to yourself, girl. You'd let him conquer your virgin territory without any kind of bargain at all.*

And that's probably the truth. Boone is *different*, and something about him makes me want to experience all the things I've been missing out on for years by being trapped in the Fishbowl.

"Whatever you want to call it, we gotta talk about the plan. I need to know what I'm walking into."

We're a few blocks away from the bar, and I glance at the clock on my phone. It's only a few minutes after ten in the morning, but that means Esteban is probably going to be pissed because I doubt Brandy got her lazy ass out of bed—if she even slept there last night—to make sure he has fresh water and food. Esteban is a demanding feathered diva when it comes to his schedule.

"Don't listen to whatever he says to you. Just grab the cage and get out of there."

We'd already argued about me helping. Boone forbade me from getting out of the car, even though my ankle is feeling a lot better this morning and the swelling has gone down. Maybe it's the painkillers talking, but I think it was a whole lot of fuss over nothing too serious.

"Why would I worry about what the bird says? I'm more concerned about someone taking a swing at my head from behind with that baseball bat you kept behind the bar."

"Brandy shouldn't be awake, if she's even there. You've got keys, and it's not like there's an alarm that's going to go off. Dad stopped paying for the monitoring before I took over managing the place."

"And no one else is going to be there?"

"No. Unless . . ."

"What?"

"When I lived above the bar and Brandy crashed there, I had a rule that she couldn't bring anyone home. If she wanted to bang some dude, she had to do it somewhere else."

"So she and her latest fuck might be upstairs."

I nod. "And Esteban isn't going to be quiet, so that could definitely wake the dead."

Boone pulls up behind the bar and shifts the car into park. "No cars here, though."

"Brandy doesn't have a car. Got repo'd a few months ago."

He just shakes his head and holds out his hand. "Keys?"

I drop the ring into his palm with the six keys to various locks in the building. "Let me help. Seriously. I'm fine. I can walk—"

Boone gives me a hard look. "Not happening. And when we get back home, your ass is going on the couch with that ankle up for the rest of the day. Get me?"

It takes everything I have not to bare my teeth at him in frustration. But I manage.

"Fine. Be a stubborn ass. Clearly, you're good at it."

He shoots me a wink. "It's your ass I'm more worried about. Got plans for that sweet peach, and I need you in full working order for them."

My mouth drops open, but Boone is out of the truck and heading for the back door of the bar before I can pull it together to respond.

That man . . .

He frustrates me and excites me in equal measure. I want to slap the smirk off his face and then kiss the crap out of him. *Yeah, I'm screwed.*

When he reaches the door, I realize I didn't tell him which key it was, but on the third try, he gets it right and the door opens.

Boone disappears inside, and now . . . I wait.

FORTY-THREE

Boone

AT TEN O'CLOCK THIS MORNING, I WAS SUPPOSED to be giving a radio interview, but I canceled it after breakfast when Ripley told me she needed to go to her friend Hope's to borrow her truck and stage a rescue operation.

Fast forward through a lot of arguing and what was probably the sexiest bargaining of my life, and here I am instead.

The bar is dark and quiet when I walk inside. The only light comes from a couple of fluorescents that I assume they keep on to deter intruders.

Didn't work on this guy.

The bird's cage is in the corner, shielded with the purple zipped cover. It's about five feet tall, three feet wide, and two feet deep. In other words, way too big for me to easily steal by myself, but whatever. I'll make it work.

When I bear-hug the cage to lift it off the stand, the bird flips out.

"*Red alert. Red alert. Danger, Will Robinson.*" The tone of his screeching changes. "*Gonna kill you, mothafucka.*"

Yeah, anyone upstairs is going to be wide awake now. I turn with the cage, glad it's not as heavy as I anticipated, and move toward the exit.

"Sorry, buddy." I use the cage to push open the door.

"*Red alert. Dead man walking.*"

As soon as I'm outside, thinking this went way more smoothly than I planned, Ripley hops out of the passenger side of the truck and hurries around to open the door to the back of the cab.

I'm cursing at her in my head as the bird swears at me to anyone who will listen.

I put the seats down in the crew cab before attempting this shit, so with the door open, all I have to do is slide the cage inside. *Thank fuck it fits.*

"Get your ass back in the car, woman. I told you—"

"You needed help."

She's more stubborn than I am, and that's saying something. I slam the door and pick Ripley up, her body pressed to mine as I walk her around the truck and heft her higher to sit her in the seat.

The bird is squawking, but I can't make out what it's saying. Either way, that's not important.

"Next time I'm kidnapping a bird for you, your ass stays in the truck. Got it?"

"Fine," she huffs. "Now we just need the stand and we can get out of here." A certain sadness shrouds her features. Probably thinking about how the life she had only days ago is nonexistent thanks to a good-for-nothing dad and a piece-of-shit cousin.

"Give me two minutes and we'll be gone. Hold tight, sugar."

I shut her door and head back into the bar. Bird-cage stand in one hand and a bag of bird food in the other, I'm ready to get out of this bar when footsteps pound down the stairs from Ripley's old apartment.

"What do you think you're doing?"

It's the cousin, Brandy. She's wearing some kind of lacy number that looks like what you'd see a stripper walk around in after she finishes dancing onstage. Not a single trace of modesty in that one, because I can see both her nipples clearly.

"Getting out of here."

She looks at the stand and the bag in my hands and then to the corner where the bird cage used to sit. Then her face twists into an ugly scowl.

"I shoulda known she'd come back for that pain-in-the-ass bird. Doesn't mean I'm gonna let you walk out of here with it, though."

"Already did, so what you gonna do about it?"

"I could call the cops on you. You'd be arrested for breaking and entering and stealing my shit. I bet those reporters would be plenty happy to pony up cash for this story too."

With one hand on the door to shove it open, I'm ready to get my ass out of this place, but when she says *pony up cash for this story too*, I still.

"What the fuck did you say?"

"That the reporters would probably be happy to pay for this story."

I drop my hand from the door and take a step toward

Brandy. She might not be the brightest bulb in the box, but even she recognizes over two hundred pounds of pissed-off man when she sees it.

"No, you said *too*. Like you've already sold them a story."

The look that flashes across her face is the epitome of *oh shit, I got caught.* But because she's the type of woman she is, Brandy decides to lie.

"I didn't do shit. You can't prove nothin'. My bitch cousin is brainwashing you."

"Shut your mouth. You don't say her name. You forget she exists. Understand? Because I can already guess what you did. You sold the story that I spent the night. Makes perfect sense now. After you shook me down for a grand and probably blew it on stupid shit, you stooped even lower to make a buck." I take another step toward her, and Brandy shrinks back instinctively before squaring her shoulders and jutting out her chin.

She drops the innocent act real quick.

"I'm not scared of you. You can't touch me. I got the number of a guy that'll pay for anything I bring him, and if you lay one hand on me, I guarantee he's gonna get the story of a lifetime." She sneers, and it's clear she feels like she has the upper hand in this situation. She's wrong.

"You think you're the first skank to threaten me with bad publicity and bullshit stories? I don't give a shit what you say about me. Go ahead and try it. I will *bury* you."

I don't know where she finds the balls, but she says, "You might not care about your reputation, but I guarantee Ripley will. You want more stories out there about how you made her your whore just like Gil Green did with her mama? Good luck gettin' her to spread her legs for you after that, *Boone.*"

My temper turns my vision red. I've never put my hands on a woman in anger, and I won't start today, but I've never met someone who pushed me this close to the limit.

"You're lucky you're not a man. I'd knock your teeth down your throat for that."

"And then I'd own your ass. Watch your step, big shot. You don't want to piss me off again." Then she decides to change her tactic. "Besides, if you're nice to me, I just might show you how much better I am than my cousin. If you want a woman who knows what she's doing, then you picked the wrong one."

Between her threats and talking shit about Ripley, I'm done holding back. "You're just a cheap slut looking for a free ride. You know how many girls like you I've met in this town? Hundreds. You're a dime a dozen. Easy come, easy go. Not worth the price of a condom I'd have to slide on my dick to make sure I don't catch whatever crotch rot you came home with last night." I lower the stand to the floor and reach into my back pocket to yank out a few hundreds before tossing them in her direction.

"That's for the bird. It's more than you'd get for a fuck, and the last cash you'll ever get out of me."

She sucks in an outraged breath, but I'm done with this bitch. I shove open the door and I'm gone.

Try selling that to the tabloids.

I work on calming my temper down, but with only fifteen feet from the back door of the bar to my truck, it ain't happening.

I yank the truck door open, shove the stand inside next to the bird who is still squawking nonsense, and slam it before climbing into the driver's seat.

"Everything okay? You were in there for longer than I thought you'd be."

"Ran into your cousin. She's fuckin' delightful. And when I say delightful, I mean I'd rather slam my dick in a door than talk to her again."

Ripley's face pales as I throw the truck in reverse. "Oh shit. What'd she say?"

"A whole lot of bullshit that ain't worth repeating."

"So it was bad? That doesn't surprise me when it comes to Brandy." Ripley's hands curl into two balled-up fists, and the bird also chimes in.

"*Dirty whore.*"

I shift into drive and pull forward. "For once, that bird has it completely right."

Ripley's gaze cuts to mine. "What do you mean? Did she . . . did she—"

"Offer to fuck me? Not exactly."

Another sharp inhale from the passenger side of the truck. "That *bitch*."

"We'll give her two more minutes of our time, and then we're done talking about her because she ain't worth it." Ripley nods and I continue. "What the hell happened between you two for her to be so damned bitter and vicious?"

Ripley's shoulders hunch forward and she wraps both arms around herself. "I wish I knew. Her dad walked out a few months after she was born, and her mom, my aunt on my mama's side, wasn't exactly a model parent. She had the same attitude—that life owed her something and didn't deliver."

"Fair enough. Subject closed." I glance in the rearview mirror and add, "Time to get this bird home."

FORTY-FOUR

Ripley

After we returned to Boone's following the Great Bird Rescue, or at least that's what I was calling it in my head, Boone put my ass on the couch, and then got Esteban settled in his huge family room.

When I told him I needed to get the bird, I hadn't really considered exactly what I was asking for. *I just moved my bird into Boone Thrasher's house. Where I'm staying temporarily.* As in, maybe for another night or two.

Hope called on the way home from the Fishbowl, but given the fact that I didn't want Boone to overhear any of the conversation we were guaranteed to have, I silenced the call and texted her to let her know I'd get back with her as soon as I could. And then I'll have to ask her if I can move Esteban to her place when I go back to crashing on the futon.

I really hope she doesn't have a problem with it. Otherwise, I'm going to be out of luck.

When Boone finishes feeding Esteban, and avoids getting pecked in the process, he pulls his phone from his pocket. "I've got about five calls to return and a radio station interview I'm two hours late for." He walks to the table, grabs the remote, and hands it to me. "I gotta handle this shit before I do anything else."

My stomach twists. "I'm so sorry. I didn't know. I never would've—"

Boone leans down and silences me with a kiss. "I do what I want, and there's nothing else I would've rather done this morning, so don't apologize. It ain't the first time I've missed something, and it won't be the last." He stands again, but tucks a stray lock of hair behind my ear. "Although I gotta say, this is the best excuse I've ever had. I'll be back in a couple hours."

He strides from the room, and I'm left alone with Esteban as he crows, "*Don't apologize.*"

"There's nothing else I would've rather done this morning."

Boone Thrasher feels like he's almost too good to be true.

I lean back on the couch and stare up at the TV screen. For the first time in longer than I can remember, I have absolutely nothing to do. I mean, I could be looking online for another part-time job, or even trying to figure out where I could possibly rent an apartment that will let me have a bird . . . but instead, I flip on the TV and cuddle into the comfortable couch, letting myself drift for a few minutes.

Maybe my life is finally turning around.

In a not-so-shocking turn of events, I discover I'm not really good at doing nothing.

When someone opens the door an hour later, I'm sitting cross-legged on a bar stool, organizing Boone's spice cupboard. I've already done the fridge and the pantry.

Call me crazy, but when I got hungry and *carefully* made my way over to the pantry to find something to eat, I was horrified at the disorganization. First, Boone has a ton of food. Probably enough to feed an army, but it was all just shoved onto the shelves in a mishmash.

My OCD tendency reared its ugly head, and while I devoured an entire bag of Lay's potato chips, I rearranged every shelf. It felt good to be somewhat useful instead of just taking up space on the couch, so I moved on to his fridge. That was a complete disaster.

Now, I've got paprika in one hand and peppercorns in the other when I hear the garage door shut and a man's footsteps coming down the hallway. He stops when he enters the kitchen carrying two giant takeout bags with a familiar yellow circle around a winged buffalo.

"What the fuck?" That's his first question when he sees my arm cocked, ready to bean him in the head with the paprika.

"Who are you?"

He's got to be at least six foot four, three hundred pounds. Basically, he's built like a linebacker, and no amount of spices would stop him if he decided to squash me like a bug.

But I'm scrappy, so I won't go down without a fight.

His eyebrows go up. "You gonna throw that at me? 'Cause my hands are kinda full right now with your lunch,

Ms. Fischer."

"How do you know my name?" My mind races to recall if I've seen this guy before, and I come up empty. "Who are you?"

"Anthony Prentiss, head of Boone's security team. And for the record, the only spice that really scares me is dill weed. Don't know what it is, but I don't want any weed in my food unless it's the good kind."

His deadpan answer knocks a chuckle loose from me. "Then you're lucky dill weed is already in the proper alphabetical order and I'm on the Ps now."

"You're a weird chick. Boone didn't mention that." He continues past me to the table where this morning we . . .

Well, suffice it to say my cheeks burn with embarrassment, but thankfully it's not like I left an ass print behind on the table.

"You hungry?" Anthony asks.

The bag of Lay's that's now empty on the counter didn't quite fill me up, and the scent of wing sauce coming from the bags has me climbing off the stool and making my way to the table.

Anthony frowns at me. "Thought you were hurt? You trying to pull some shit over on my man, Boone? Because if you are, I'll make sure you regret it."

I plop down on one of the chairs and lift my ankle for him to inspect. The bruising is a lovely mix of black and purple today. "It looks worse than it feels, at least with the ibuprofen. As long as I don't try to dance an Irish jig, I'm pretty sure walking on it isn't going to kill me."

With his frown still firmly in place, Anthony lifts a takeout container from the bag. "Boone ain't gonna be happy to see you walking around. He said he didn't even want you trying crutches, so I didn't bring any."

My eyes widen. "Are you kidding me? What does he expect me to do? Levitate to the bathroom if he can't carry me?"

Anthony winces. "I'm guessing he didn't think it all the way through. He's just worried about you. Thinks all this shit is his fault."

"I appreciate the concern, but I'm really okay. Seriously. Providing you don't take the drugs away, it just aches a little." I scan the containers as he continues to lift them out of the bags. "Did you bring enough for the entire band? Because this seems a little excessive for only a couple people."

"Boone likes leftovers. Says he wrote some of his best songs eatin' cold wings, so the man gets all the wings so he can eat 'em cold later."

Interesting. That's a little quirk I knew nothing about, but then again, there's a lot I don't know about Boone. I decide to go on a fact-finding mission.

"How old is he?"

Anthony's gaze cuts to me. "You haven't googled him?" When I shake my head, he looks truly surprised. "Shit, woman. You gotta be the only bitch ever been in his bed who hasn't."

I raise a hand. "Don't call me a bitch. I don't like it."

Anthony shrugs. "Didn't mean no disrespect."

I shake it off. "I know, but I'd appreciate if you substitute some other word in the future."

Before he responds, the back door shuts again and Boone appears in the breakfast nook, or really cavern, because it's a huge chunk of the room.

"Thanks, man. You always know what I like." Boone moves to stand behind me and drops his hands onto my shoulders. "You keep yourself entertained and off your ankle like a good girl?"

I open my mouth to tell the tiniest white lie, but Anthony beats me.

"When I came in, she was alphabetizing your spice cupboard." He jerks his shoulder toward the kitchen, and Boone takes in the bar stool and mess of bottles on the counter that he walked by moments ago without noticing.

His hands tighten on my shoulders. "Ripley . . ."

I crane my head around to look at him. "It's not like you can expect me to sit on the couch and do nothing for hours. I'm pretty sure I don't actually know how to do nothing. I'm used to being busy."

Boone shakes his head and leans down to whisper in my ear. "You know how I mentioned I had plans for that amazing ass of yours? Now they include leaving my handprint on it to get my point across."

My eyes go wide, and I glance at Anthony to see if he heard. Either he didn't or he's skilled at pretending.

When I don't respond, Boone squeezes my shoulders again and drags his lips to my temple to press a kiss there.

He steps back and scans the containers. "What kind of wings do you want? We've got Caribbean jerk, Asian, hot, honey barbecue, and habanero."

"Habanero and hot."

He glances back at me. "The fact that you like 'em spicy shouldn't surprise me at all."

I don't know what that's supposed to mean, but he

loads up my plate and invites Anthony to eat with us.

There's something about Boone inviting an employee to join us in mowing down this feast that hits me square in the chest. It's one more instance of my preconceived notions being systematically proven wrong.

Don't get me wrong, Boone's still an arrogant asshole sometimes, but he's not the entitled man diva I expected.

Anthony sits at the table like he's done it hundreds of times before, and I'm guessing he has. Watching their interaction and how they rib each other, it's clear that he isn't solely an employee to Boone. He's also a friend.

"So, you get those interviews knocked out?" Anthony asks.

I'm curious about this too, because I felt like shit that Boone missed something because of me.

A pissed-off expression flashes across Boone's features before he wipes it away. "Yeah, I did. But I'm telling Nick and Charity that I'm done with them if they can't leave the personal questions out of it. I'm there to talk about my music, and that's it."

Anthony glances at me, and heat works its way up my neck to my cheeks. *Were they questions about me or about the ex? Or both?* I'd put my money on the last.

The head of security changes the subject. "You got plans for the rest of the day? Writing?"

I assume writing means writing songs, and my assumption is confirmed when Boone shrugs.

"Nah. Not feeling the words right now. I'm still finding my rhythm for these last few." His attention shifts to me. "I was thinking I'd set up some targets and see if this city girl can shoot."

My eyebrows climb up my forehead. “Say what now?”

“You and me and a couple of long guns on the porch. You’re in the country; you gotta do some country shit. And I can guarantee you won’t be walking all over the house on that ankle.”

“I’m fine. I swear. It barely even hurts.”

“Because you took pain meds. That doesn’t mean you’re all better, sugar. You gotta take it easy.”

“The doctor said a few days. Tomorrow is basically three days, and it’s already afternoon, so I’m pretty much there.” My argument may be ridiculous, but it’s the only one I’ve got. “Besides, I’ll go stir crazy if you expect me to sit on that couch all day eating bonbons. I’m not that kind of girl.”

A smile twitches the edge of his mouth. “I figured that out.” He trades a meaningful look with Anthony, and I have no idea what kind of silent conversation they’re having.

When we finish eating, Boone and Anthony carry the containers of leftovers to the fridge, and Anthony bursts out laughing when he opens the door.

Boone spins around to look at me. “What the hell happened to my fridge?”

FORTY-FIVE

Boone

RIPLEY IS A NUT, BUT DAMNED IF I DON'T LIKE HER exactly that way. I leave the girl for a couple of hours, and instead of taking it easy, she reorganized most of my kitchen.

I can't help but picture Amber in the same situation. She wouldn't have moved her ass off the couch. She would have called me every five minutes to fetch and carry for her. I would have wanted to strangle her within a half hour because of the constant interruptions. If one hundred percent of my attention wasn't fixed on her whenever we were in the same place, she'd stage a snit fit to end all snit fits.

At the time, I'd just assumed that's what you had to put up with when you were with someone long-term, like embracing their flaws with their strengths, but now I know that's total bullshit.

Amber was probably a little bit of a bitch.

Ripley, on the other hand, is a straight-up nut.

I'll take a nut over a bitch any day, even though she's

staring at the .22 in my hands like it's going to jump up and bite her.

"*Don't shoot. Don't shoot*," Esteban squawks through the open window where he watches from his cage.

"Zip it, bird," I say over my shoulder before looking back at Ripley. "You ever shoot a gun before?"

She shakes her head, still warily eying the Winchester rifle.

"Then it's about time you learn. Never know when you might need the skill."

"Maybe we could try something smaller first?"

"Like a BB gun? Because that's about all that's gonna be smaller. Maybe a pellet gun." I take in her expression. "You scared?"

That question has Ripley straightening her shoulders in no time. "Of course not."

"That's what I thought. Time to learn to shoot."

Anthony went out after we were done eating and put targets up in all the usual places, including a few closer ones for Ripley to start with. Is that really part of his job as head of security? Nope, but he does it anyway because he's a cool guy, even though he's got his hands full with managing the rest of my security issues, including running down any and all possible threats that come through my e-mail and other fan mail. It's not a small job. Apparently a lot of people think I'm an asshole.

Maybe subconsciously, that's why I want to know Ripley can handle a gun. I've only had one crazy ass actually make an attempt to shoot me, but you never know what could happen with the whack jobs out there.

"Let's make a wager. You hit three targets in a row

before we're done, and I'll eat your pussy until you come three times. Hard."

It's not really much of a wager because I'm planning on doing it anyway, but Ripley doesn't know that. She shifts in the deck chair I pulled up for her, and I bet she's getting wet.

I love that, for the record.

"That way you'll be all sweet and relaxed for me before I play with your ass."

Her gaze darts to mine. "We're . . . you mean . . . tonight?"

I wink. "We're just getting started. Don't worry, we'll take it slow."

She mumbles something under her breath, and it sounds like *how am I supposed to concentrate now?*

"All right, watch me demonstrate." After going through all the parts of the gun and showing her how everything works, including the safety, I hand her some ear protectors and start popping off rounds, causing four of the targets to spin.

Her eyes are wide when I lower the rifle and engage the safety.

"You're good at that." She yells the words because her ears are covered, and it's really fucking cute.

I remove my ear protectors and lift hers off too. "Sugar, I'm as redneck as it gets. Just because I got money doesn't mean I've changed who I really am."

"I like that about you."

It might not seem like much in the way of compliments, but it's sincere, and knowing about Ripley and her past, it's pretty huge to me.

"There's a hell of a lot I like about you, Ripley Fischer. Now, it's your turn. Put the muffs back on and get ready to kick some target ass."

FORTY-SIX

Ripley

"THERE'S A HELL OF A LOT *I* LIKE ABOUT YOU, *Ripley Fischer*."

I swear, at least fifty percent of what comes out of Boone Thrasher's mouth makes me want to jump him. How does he do that?

He even looks as sexy as hell shooting that gun, which is something I never thought in my entire life about another human being, even a hot actor on TV.

When I take the gun from him, my nerves ratchet up to red-alert levels. Ma and Gil were shot. They were both dead in minutes, the coroner's report said.

"You okay?" Boone asks.

I snap out of my thoughts and back to the present.

"Yeah. Fine." I know I'm yelling, but I don't care. If I talk quietly, I can't even hear myself.

Boone helps me position the rifle against my shoulder. I look down the sight like he explained, bringing the little metal part on the tip between the two metal pieces closer to me. When I've got a round orange target sighted in, I squeeze the trigger.

I jerk at the *pop*, but the target doesn't spin like Boone's did.

"You scared yourself. Anticipating the recoil. But now you know there really isn't one, so you can calm down and nail that target. Got it?"

Boone speaks loudly enough that I can hear him through my ear protection, and I nod.

For some strange reason, even though I wasn't really keen on doing this, now I'm determined. I want to hit that damn target.

It has nothing to do with the orgasms he promised me.

Okay, that's a lie.

I focus on the same target and take a deep breath after I line up the sight, letting it out before I squeeze the trigger. I don't know where the bullet hits but the target spins, indicating I made contact. I raise my head.

"I did it!"

Boone takes the rifle from my hands and engages the safety before kissing the crap out of me.

"That's my girl," he says, quietly enough that I almost can't hear him through the muffs.

Warmth slides through my chest, and it scares the ever-loving hell out of me.

I like him. A lot.

Boone keeps me at the target shooting until my stomach grumbles, but I still haven't hit my three targets in a row. I can nail two, but then I choke up and freeze on the third.

He taps me on the shoulder after the last time I pull the trigger and there's only a click.

"Let's pack it up and go eat some of those leftover wings. I can't have you starving out here."

I lift the earmuff off one ear. "Do you have more bullets? I'm going one more time."

Boone's dark eyebrow rises and he studies me. "Is that right?"

I nod.

"You know I'm gonna make you come hard regardless? Because, sugar, you're the sexiest thing I've ever seen in my life when you finally let down your guard." That warm feeling burns hot again. "Especially when I'm looking at your face from between your legs." Boone winks.

The warm feeling doesn't fade when he turns into a smartass. It morphs into flames between my thighs.

Boone Thrasher is dangerous . . . in the best way possible.

"Bullets," I say, holding out a hand.

"Anyone ever told you that you're more stubborn than a mule?" Instead of holding out his hand for me to give him the magazine like he had the rest of the afternoon, he drops ten rounds in my hand.

"I don't think anyone I know has ever owned a mule."

"My folks used to have one at their place. They adopted it from some farmer who was going to sell it to the glue factory or some shit like that, and my ma wouldn't stand for it after she heard about it. Got my daddy up at dawn to go down and bargain with the old man. Ma sat in the truck with a shotgun in her lap, just in case he wouldn't deal, at least according to my dad."

"She sounds feisty."

A smile stretches over Boone's face. "She sure is. Best woman I've ever known. Call me a mama's boy if you want, but I owe that woman everything." He watches as I load the magazine with painstaking care. "You'll have to take a ride down there with me and meet them. They'd like you. Ma would recognize a kindred spirit."

My hand shakes when he talks about me meeting his folks. Like this is something more than me being the rebound after his relationship with his ex-girlfriend went balls up in the most spectacular fashion.

"They sound like great people." I shove the magazine back into place, readjust my ear protection, and lift the rifle to my shoulder. "It's game time," I whisper to myself as I aim at the first target.

It's shaped like a squirrel, and I've been getting lucky with it all day.

Sorry, Mr. Squirrel. You're only plastic. I wouldn't shoot you in real life.

I squeeze the trigger and pop off the first round.

Hit! The squirrel spins on his metal frame.

Boone's cheer comes from beside me, and I have to fight to keep my concentration instead of letting my triumphant smile loose. *No celebrating until it's done and won.*

I move on to target number two, this one some kind of rodent. I slow my breathing and squeeze.

Hit! Inside, I do a little dance, but I make no outward sign of my excitement because I've already gotten this far a couple of times.

Keep your expectations low, Rip. Isn't that what life has taught you? Best way to avoid disappointment.

Depressing words, but true.

I find target number three. It's a rabbit. I've missed it four or five times. Maybe because I think rabbits are super cute and I wanted one from the pet store when I was seven, but Pop said no way would he let that thing in the apartment. I almost switch back to the squirrel, something I know I can hit, but I'm determined. What's the point of winning if I don't do it in a way that means something?

Setting my sights on the rabbit, I picture the little furry bastard flipping me off and mocking me for all my misses. *Not so cute now, asshole.*

I hold my breath as I pull the trigger. *It spins!*

My finger slams over the safety, engaging it before I jump out of my seat and toss off my earmuffs. Boone takes the rifle from my hand, sets it aside, and clutches me around the waist to lift me in the air over his head and twirl me around in a circle.

"One hell of a shot for someone who's never picked up a rifle in her life. Damn, sugar, that was badass."

He lowers me, letting my front slide down his entire body. The heat that had bloomed between my legs is back.

I want him. I try to piece together the words in my head to tell him, stumbling over something so simple, and then I lose my chance because my stomach growls again.

Boone carries me into the house.

"First, I'm gonna deliver on those promises, then we're gonna get some of those leftover wings together and go for a ride. I got something I want to show you."

FORTY-SEVEN

Boone

I lower Ripley onto the seat of the ATV, strap down our food in the rack at the back, and settle myself right behind her, lifting her onto my lap.

She's the perfect size to fit there, with the luscious curve of her ass pressing against my dick.

Is there anything this woman could do that wouldn't turn me on? I suspect the answer to that question is a solid *no*.

Once again, I can't help but think of the one time I tried to get Amber to go out on an ATV with me to see my property. She'd looked at me like I'd asked her to walk through a pit of vipers. She was an LA girl, and not interested in learning about the country way of life. At least, not the part that was the real me.

Even now that she's out of my life, she's still causing me grief. When I was putting up the rifle, my phone wouldn't stop pinging with texts from Nick. Amber is back in Nashville, making demands and causing trouble.

Just what I don't need right now . . . so I left my phone in the house because I wasn't about to let her ruin this night.

Ripley's practically vibrating with excitement. She turns her head to the side. "Are you going to let me drive? Or are you one of those guys who won't let a woman do it when you're around?"

As much as I want to say no way in hell am I letting her drive because she's never been on an ATV before, I know she's fully capable. My five-year-old nephew can run around the yard on his.

"How about on the way back?"

"Deal."

Something about Ripley makes me wonder what it would be like to make a lot more deals with her. I told myself she was a distraction in the beginning. Someone to take my mind off the fact that Amber fucked me over so hard, but that didn't last long.

Hell, the first time I got my hands on Ripley, I knew this was something else. Having her in my house, fitting into my life so easily, drives it home.

My future with Amber was always a hazy concept. I couldn't picture her walking down the aisle of a simple country church to meet me at the front while my family gathered around. I couldn't see us arguing about what to name a kid, or her trying to talk me out of splurging on Christmas toys so our kids wouldn't be spoiled brats.

All I could see with Amber was walking down a red carpet while she posed and cameras flashed around us, or maybe sitting next to her at an awards show. Maybe that's because when I look back on it, I realize we didn't do a lot more than that together.

But Ripley? She slides into all the other scenes I've pictured having in my life like she was always meant to be there. It should scare the ever-living hell out of me, but it doesn't.

I've learned a lot of things in my life already, including the fact that shit happens for a reason, even when you don't know why at the time. My brother got half his leg blown off in Afghanistan, and there was nothing that could make me understand why that had to happen. But fate had me there on a USO tour at the same time, and I was able to be by his side in Germany as they fought to save his life.

And when he came home early, frustrated and cursing fate for condemning him to this life, he met his wife while she was visiting her brother at Walter Reed. He tells it as love at first sight. She says he was doped up on painkillers, but either way, now they have an amazing boy, another on the way, and a house down the road from my parents.

The worst thing to happen in his life led him to the best thing. You can't tell me that wasn't meant to be.

I'm hoping life has a similar plan in store for me. The darkest moment taking me down a path that leads me to the light.

"Are we gonna ride this thing or what, superstar?" Ripley wiggles her ass on my lap, the excitement in her tone loud and clear.

I wrap my fist around her ponytail and tug it to one side as I lean forward, dragging my teeth down the tendon of her neck before adding some pressure at the curve of her shoulder.

Ripley inhales harshly before squirming again, this

time for a completely different reason.

"First, we're gonna ride *this thing*, and then I'm gonna ride you."

She arches back, unable to move because of my grip on her hair. "Is that right?"

"Damn right."

A shiver ripples through her body.

"You wet, sugar?"

"You'll have to wait to find that out for yourself."

Her words goad me into firing up the ATV. I wrap an arm around her waist and pull her back so she's flush against me.

"Hold on tight." I give it some gas and steer us toward our destination.

Fifteen minutes later, I stop the ATV beside my stocked pond. Sure, I took a longer route than usual to get here, but that's because I wasn't ready to let Ripley off my lap.

She sucks in an audible breath when she sees the little dock that stops thirty feet into the twenty-acre pond as the sun starts sinking in an explosion of reds, oranges, and yellows.

"It's beautiful here."

"Glad you like it. We're gonna have us a picnic."

Ripley twists around to look at me. "I never would've guessed that you were a picnic kind of guy."

The breeze catches a piece of her hair that pulled free of her ponytail, and I brush it away from her face. Even though the weather hasn't taken much of a chill, I'm glad I grabbed a blanket to bring along with us.

"A beautiful woman, a trout pond, a sunset, and cold wings? Those are some of my favorite things. Put 'em all together and it's the perfect evening."

FORTY-EIGHT

Ripley

JUST LIKE THAT, BOONE CRUSHES MY REMAINING preconceived notions.

When he climbs off the ATV, he leaves me on the seat. "Hold tight a second. Let me get this set up, and then I'll bring you down."

"I can walk, superstar. For real. My ankle feels way better."

He gives me a pointed look. "Tomorrow. Take one more night to let it heal up, and then we'll talk about it."

When is the last time anyone cared this much or worried about me like this?

Maybe my mama when I broke my wrist falling down the stairs when I was six? Definitely not Pop. He complained about me being clumsy and running up doctor bills. Of course, he didn't see the irony when he fell down the same stairs drunk and ended up in surgery with loads more bills that I got stuck paying for.

Boone takes a blanket, spreads it out at the end of the

dock, and sits the bag of takeout on it before coming back for me.

"My dad used to take me fishing when I was a kid, and sometimes, if I was lucky, my granddad would come too. Always at the crack of dawn. I never wanted to get up that early, but I also wasn't gonna miss a chance to hang out with them."

He keeps talking as he lifts me into his arms and carries me to the blanket.

"Granddad had a pond double this size on his property, and we'd all sit on the end of the dock, or sometimes pile into an old rowboat and head out to the middle. Dad would critique my casting, showing me how to do it better, and then Granddad would critique his teaching method and show us both how to perfect it."

I can picture a little boy with Boone's dark hair and blue eyes watching raptly as the two most important men in his life passed down their knowledge.

"That sounds like an amazing way to grow up."

Boone lowers me to the blanket at the end of the dock where my feet dangle over the edge, and joins me. The water is low enough that I can't touch it, but not so low that I can't see the little disturbances in the surface where bugs land and fish come up to the surface to try to grab them.

"It was. We'd haul in as many fish as we could, keeping count of who had the most. Granddad always won, for the record. Then we'd take 'em back to the house and my mom would be there with Granny T, and they'd wait for us to filet 'em all and then fry up a whole mess of them. We'd eat outside on the picnic table, drinking sweet tea and eating whatever vegetables had come from the garden that day."

The picture Boone paints of his childhood is . . . perfect.

"That sounds incredible. Like something straight out of a movie."

Boone chuckles as he hands me a container of wings. "I wouldn't say that. There was plenty of stuff that wasn't perfect. Trying to pull together the money to buy new shingles to fix the roof one summer because Ma didn't have any more pots and pans to catch the drips. I tried to quit guitar lessons so they could put the money toward the roof, but Ma wouldn't let me. Instead, she traded out preserves for Mrs. Winston, the high school music teacher, to start me on the piano too. I thought Dad was gonna be pissed, but he wasn't. He just told me that learning every skill that came my way was the smartest thing I could do to make a better future for myself."

I swallow back the lump in my throat. What I remember most is Mama and me trying to dodge Pop's slaps for things we didn't do well enough, and Pop putting me to work as soon as I was big enough to haul a case of beer. She'd argued with him about that, but it ended with her having a split lip and me working.

Other than going to school, I barely set foot outside the Fishbowl and our apartment while growing up. Maybe it was better that way. Less chance for people to ask about the bruises.

A wave of sadness threatens to overwhelm me, so I turn the conversation back to Boone.

"You still close with your folks?"

Boone, in the middle of chewing, nods and finishes before he answers. "Definitely. I see them as often as I can.

They're the most real people in my life."

"What do you mean?" I ask before diving into my own wings.

"You can tell I didn't grow up with money. We had a whole lot of love, but not a lot of extras. I didn't want for anything, though. They found a way to make sure I had what I needed, and I didn't ask for more than that. They're the same way now. They wouldn't dream of asking me for something. No one in my family expects handouts. Shit, I had to pay off my parents' mortgage in secret because they wouldn't take the check I wrote from my first record deal. I tried to buy my dad a new truck but he told me no, his old one was still running fine." Boone pauses and laughs. "He'll be surprised when one shows up for his birthday this year, though, whether he wants it or not."

Along with the warmth that accompanies the vision of Boone's dad getting a new truck comes a wave of despair. Will the last words Pop ever speaks to me be the ones in anger? Then again, when was the last time he actually said something kind?

I search my memory, and all I can find is criticism about how I ran the bar and didn't make enough money, or some other negative thing he found to complain about.

The shaft of pain that stabs me through the heart is regret for the relationship I'll never have with either of my parents.

"And Ma," Boone continues. "She's always wanted a convertible. She'd deny it as being too impractical, but I've seen the way she looks at them, especially in those old movies she loves where the women wrap their hair in a scarf so the wind doesn't mess it up. I should wait until

Christmas, but then the roads might not cooperate, so she's getting her convertible when Dad gets his truck. And a whole box of scarves wrapped up in the front seat."

He's buying his mother scarves for her hair for her convertible. I squeeze my eyes shut at the sting of tears springing forth at the thoughtfulness of the gesture. *Boone Thrasher is a good man.* And yet, I feel like not many people really know the truth about him.

"How did anyone ever paint you as the bad boy of country music?" I ask.

He leans back on the dock and glances at me before staring off into the sunset.

"Don't get the idea that I'm some sort of saint, sugar. I've done plenty of shit I shouldn't have. Especially when I first started riding that wave of fame. It's a crazy world out there. Not only does everyone want something from you, but all of a sudden, the barriers start coming down."

"Barriers?"

"The roadblocks to all the things you wanted that you couldn't have before. The money, the cars, the houses, the women, the fans, the venues, the interviews. It's all there, just waiting for you to take what you want from it. And then there's the booze and the drugs, and God knows none of that shit mixes well together."

"I can't even imagine what that would be like."

Boone turns back to me. "It's a blessing and a curse. I wouldn't trade this life for anything, except for maybe to have my privacy and anonymity back. You've already seen it. It's hard to make a move without someone saying something about it, or the press getting wind of it and twisting it into something it isn't. Then you've got the pressure to put out another number-one hit, a platinum album, a sold-out show . . ."

These are all things I never would have really considered, but he's right. When you think about how famous musicians live, it's easy to only think about the good parts, and not the crushing responsibilities and expectations that go along with it.

"How do you handle it?"

Boone smiles but it's a little lopsided, and something about it makes me want to kiss it off his face.

"At first, I loved every second, but when it started to get old, there was a lot of booze, women, and drugs. And there were some fights . . . My brother kicked my ass when he showed up at a show, and I was high as a kite and barely recognized him. He reminded me that what I have is a privilege and I needed to be smart about it. I'm not saying I don't still get high on occasion, but it's nothing like the road I was on for a bit."

My eyes must be wide because Boone adds, "Don't look so surprised. You know I'm no Boy Scout."

I shake my head. "That's not why I'm surprised. It's just you sound so self-aware about it all."

This time he laughs, and it's a genuine one. "Because I am. I've got a family that keeps me grounded and stops me from screwing up too bad. And then I've got moments like this, when I can get away from being Boone Thrasher, country music's bad boy, and just be Boone. Catching my own dinner, cleaning it, and cooking it has a tendency to remind me that even though some things have changed, I'm still the same redneck I've always been." He shoots me a wink. "Although my kitchen's a little fancier these days, the fish still tastes the same."

I can't help but voice the thought I had earlier. "You're a good man, Boone."

His smile takes on a wicked edge. "I might be a good man, but I want to do very bad things to you."

That heat between my legs flares into a rush of need. With my fingers sticky from wings, I lean forward and press a kiss to his lips. My voice is husky when I speak again.

"Good. I can't wait."

Boone deepens the kiss, and I'm wondering if we're going to get naked right on this dock, but the sound of another ATV coming toward the pond breaks us apart.

"What the fuck?"

A headlight cuts through the dusk, shining on us.

"Boone! You gotta come back to the house. We got a big fucking problem," Anthony yells.

"What kind of problem?"

"The cops. They're here with a warrant for your arrest."

Boone and Ripley's story concludes in

REAL SEXY

Click on www.meghanmarch.com/#!newsletter/c1uhp to sign up for my newsletter, and never miss another announcement about upcoming projects, new releases, sales, exclusive excerpts, and giveaways.

I'd love to hear what you thought about *Real Dirty!* If you have a few moments to leave a review on the retailer's site where you purchased the book, I'd be incredibly grateful. Send me a link at meghanmarchbooks@gmail.com, and I'll thank you with a personal note.

ALSO BY MEGHAN MARCH

Take Me Back

Bad Judgment

Beneath Series:
Beneath These Shadows
Beneath This Mask
Beneath This Ink
Beneath These Chains
Beneath These Scars
Beneath These Lies

Flash Bang Series:
Flash Bang
Hard Charger

Dirty Billionaire Trilogy:
Dirty Billionaire
Dirty Pleasures
Dirty Together

Dirty Girl Duet:
Dirty Girl
Dirty Love

Real Duet:
Real Good Man
Real Good Love

Real Dirty Duet:
Real Dirty
Real Sexy

ACKNOWLEDGMENTS

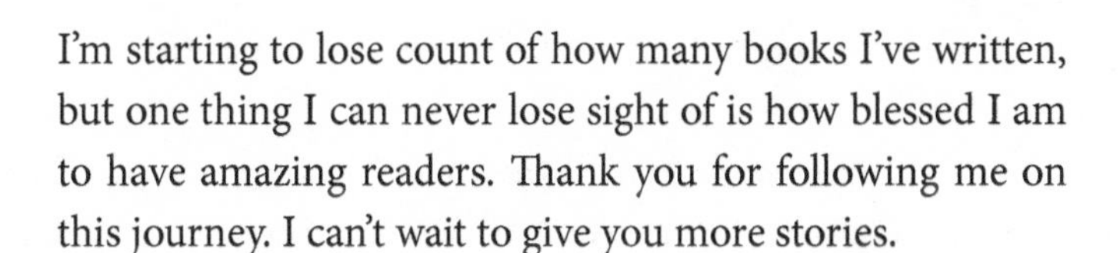

I'm starting to lose count of how many books I've written, but one thing I can never lose sight of is how blessed I am to have amazing readers. Thank you for following me on this journey. I can't wait to give you more stories.

To my entire team, I love you all, and I couldn't do this without you. Let's keep doing this for a long, long time, okay?

AUTHOR'S NOTE

I'd love to hear from you. Connect with me at:

Website: www.meghanmarch.com
Facebook: www.facebook.com/MeghanMarchAuthor
Twitter: www.twitter.com/meghan_march
Instagram: www.instagram.com/meghanmarch

Meghan March

UNAPOLOGETICALLY SEXY ROMANCE

ABOUT THE AUTHOR

Meghan March has been known to wear camo face paint and tromp around in the woods wearing mud-covered boots, all while sporting a perfect manicure. She's also impulsive, easily entertained, and absolutely unapologetic about the fact that she loves to read and write smut.

Her past lives include slinging auto parts, selling lingerie, making custom jewelry, and practicing corporate law. Writing books about dirty-talking alpha males and the strong, sassy women who bring them to their knees is by far the most fabulous job she's ever had.

She loves hearing from her readers at meghanmarchbooks@gmail.com.

CPSIA information can be obtained
at www.ICGtesting.com
Printed in the USA
FSHW022033200220
67379FS